THE THRILL BOOK

Issued Semimonthly. Application made for entry as Second-class Matter at the Post Office, New York, N. Y., by STREET & SMITH, 79-89 7th Ave., New York. Copyright, 1919, by STREET & SMITH CORPORATION.   YEARLY SUBSCRIPTION, $2.00.

Vol. I.   No. 1.   New York, March 1, 1919.   Price Ten Cents.

Wolf of the Steppes
By Greye La Spina

Letter from Doctor Thomas Connors to Amdi Rubdah, the adept, Teheran, Persia.

TO my dear Master, greetings:
Not in vain have I learned from you somewhat of the mysteries enveloping the human soul in its earth life. In my performance for the first time of the ancient incantations you taught me under the Persian stars, I have gained a vivid knowledge of the occult powers resident in the flesh-caged spirit of man and realize with rejoicing the impotence of Evil in the everlasting conflict with Truth, especially when that Truth is armed with the knowledge that is power.

In this packet I inclose a number of letters sent me by my friend and colleague, Doctor Greeley. They will serve as an introduction to my narrative, which will follow, and they will bring you to the evening of the day I arrived at my friend's house.

Extract from letter of Doctor Andrew Greeley to Doctor Thomas Connors.

Since I penned the above memoranda regarding the solvent you inquired about, I have had an adventure, a very romantic adventure for an elderly married man! It really should have been a young bachelor like yourself, Tom, to have gone gallantly to the rescue. Myra has become so fond of our heroine that she insists that we should adopt the young lady. Of course this would be out of the question until we knew more about the girl.

Now I suppose I may as well satisfy your curiosity. About two weeks ago I was motoring out toward Riverside about dusk to look in on a convalescing patient. As I approached the grounds of a large, handsome residence which I had observed more than once when passing, I heard suddenly a long-drawn-out whining on a quavering and eerie note that was most unpleasant; it changed at last into an undulation that sent my blood cold. So unusual was the howl

that involuntarily I slowed the car to listen, in case the animal should give voice again.

I would have stopped entirely, had not a white figure with frantically waving arms sprung out of the hedge and charged upon me, springing on the running board with an agility and an indifference to danger that startled me. It was a young and very good-looking girl. Such fear stared at me out of her wild eyes that when she clambered in beside me and commanded me to go on I did not hesitate, but obeyed her agonized cry.

"For God's sake don't stop!" she flung at me. "If you value your life, go on quickly!"

With that I heard the crashing of a heavy body through the shrubbery, and looked back with a thrill of apprehension to see a pair of flaming red eyes coming toward us at such a speed that I stood not on the order of my going. I shot out of there, the little flivver snorting like a mad thing, while that weird howl wailed out behind us. Why on earth I should have had such a horror of that great dog I don't know, unless the girl's terror had infected me, but I certainly felt as if the devil himself were swinging along after us. I turned toward home at the first side road, and am under the impression that the beast only dropped behind when we got into the village; I can assure you I didn't stop to look behind me after that last glance.

My wife was much astonished at her husband's return with a fainting heroine, and she had her hands full, the girl going into one attack of hysterics after another. All that we could get out of her during the next few days was that her name is Vera Andrevik;

that she is an orphan; and that it will be useless for us to ask further explanations from her. She insists upon the last point with a firmness as strong as it is inexplicable, for naturally much depends upon it in her own interests.

Until she has become more normal we must content ourselves with the meager information she has condescended to give us. Her strange whims occupy us at present, giving much food for thought. In spite of the sultry nights now, she will not sleep until both windows in her room are locked and the Venetian blinds drawn and fastened. She makes a complete tour of the house nightly, personally superintending the securing of downstairs windows and doors. Lastly she locks herself into her room. Her mysterious precautions have furnished Myra and me the most lively curiosity.

If you happen to hear of a lovely lost Russian heiress, let me hear from you at once! On the other hand, if you are asked about the whereabouts of a fair but mentally unbalanced young lady, communicate with me also. As ever,   ANDREW.

Letter from Doctor Greeley to Doctor Connors, dated the week after the preceding letter.

DEAR TOM: Since writing you last our strange visitor has been acting in such an odd manner that I don't know but that you'd better come over when you get a chance and give me your opinion as to her sanity. My wife declares the girl as sane as I am, but you know Myra; everything is to her what she wants it to be.

Vera Andrevik has told us nothing more than I wrote you last. I ventured one evening to ask if she couldn't give us her mother's address; she turned absolutely white, looked at me with such a *ghastly* expression of horror that I was much startled; then she fell back limply in a faint. Myra, of course, scolded me for my masculine abruptness; she thinks I should leave the management of the matter to her entirely. We are agreed that it will not be wise to question the girl yet, as it will take time for her to regain her supposedly normal nervous condition. But you can judge from the foregoing if the subjects of home and mother are taboo or not.

I mentioned casually to Myra, in Vera's presence, a half-formed intention to make inquiries at the residence where the dog belonged. Vera flung herself at my feet in an agony of terror, hysterically begging me not to enter the grounds there. She declared that she could not explain, but that if I did not follow her counsel I would bring such peril upon us all as I could not imagine in my wildest flights of fancy. I promised not to go, but not entirely on account of Vera's pleas and representations; I have felt such a growing horror of that place that I can't bring myself to go down the road in front of it. For a gray-haired old doctor that's going some, isn't it? The red-eyed dog's howl has affected me most unpleasantly.

In the meantime, our visitor refused to go out of the house except in the flivver, and then she wraps herself around with thick veils, regardless of the sweltering heat of these close days. At night she continues to lock herself into her room. When I remonstrate with her she says: "Do you suppose I like to do it, Doctor Andrew? Yet it must be done." She refuses

to enlighten me further; she says she doesn't care to be considered a harmless lunatic. I feel like telling her that she acts fairly crazy as it is to shut herself up on hot nights without outside air, but what's the use?

I am positive that she has been under a nervous strain that has for the time being unhinged her mind. Come out when you can, Tom, and observe the case. I shall be deeply interested to know what you think about it. But, for the love of mercy, don't come blundering into the house without letting me know first! The bell has been muffled because Vera nearly has convulsions every time it rings, such is her terror of God knows what. She would probably go into a cataleptic fit if she happened to see you come into the house unannounced. Yours,   ANDREW.

From the same to the same.

DEAR TOM: I gather, from the pronouncedly mystical tone of your last letter, that you've been dabbling again in the forbidden arts, seeking for the unfindable secrets of the soul. Let 'em alone, boy; they never brought good to any one, and it's dangerous business, most unsettling to the brain.

Instead of puzzling out magic spells, come down for a few days and help me work out a few chemical problems in my laboratory. It's been a long time since you've helped me with research work.

I've another reason for wanting you here, and that —as you may have surmised—is Vera. Tom, that child is suffering terribly. Unless she can relieve her mind I fear she will permanently lose her mental poise. She declares she is as sane as we are, but says she cannot tell us the story that would throw light on her queer actions, because, if she did, we would believe her insane. Then she just sobs and sobs, and it is all Myra can do to keep her from going into hysterics.

To-day she almost went into a spasm in the automobile, and for almost nothing. She and Myra were in the back seat. A chap just wandered right into the path of the car, and when I stopped the old flivver with a jerk he looked at Vera and smiled in a triumphant manner that was highly unpleasant. He was an odd-looking fellow; wore a gray fur-trimmed overcoat and a gray fur cap, from under which his long, straight hair escaped in wild confusion. His heavy, black eyebrows met in a nearly horizontal line across his forehead, giving him a strangely fierce expression which his eyes did not contradict; I thought the latter looked almost garnet in color, an impression which Myra verified. The hand nearest us was hooked carelessly into his coat pocket by the thumb, and of the four fingers hanging outside the pocket the forefinger was so long that the abnormality was very pronounced; I have never seen such a strange hand before.

Vera began to whimper, clutching at Myra as if in abject, uncontrollable fear. "Go on, go on!" she cried wildly to me.

I had no good reason not to humor her, especially as the man finally stepped out of our way. He stood there, deliberately reading our license number aloud; Myra heard him after we had passed. Now why on earth should he do that? It was entirely his own fault that he had gotten in the way, and the old flivver never so much as touched him.

All the way home Vera moaned and carried on in the most pitiful manner, imploring us not to let "him" take her away from us. Her heartrending pleas to Mrs. Myra, as she calls my wife—for she never uses the word "mother"—were enough to draw tears to the eyes of a stone image. Myra assured her that no one should take her away against her own will, and she finally quieted down. But we had a bad night with her afterward, for at dusk some confounded dog came into our garden and took to howling, and it got on my nerves to such an extent that I actually imagined I recognized the howl of my friend of the red eyes, of whom I wrote you previously.

Vera went into a frenzy of terror at the sound of those howls, and insisted upon going the rounds of the doors and windows with my wife to assure herself that everything was securely fastened. Her fear is infectious; both Myra and I have impatiently assured each other numberless times that we do not feel in the least wrought up nervously, but the fact that we have had to affirm our mental calm is sufficient evidence that that confounded dog's howling and Vera's groundless fears have together broken in upon our sleep sufficiently to start us both well on the way to nervous trouble.

I am beginning to connect Vera's terror definitely with the fierce dog that chased my car that first night; just what the connection is I cannot figure out now, but the solution may present itself unexpectedly. What complicates matters is the effect upon Vera of that stranger who practically held up our car this morning; can he have something to do with the mystery also? Yours, ANDREW.

Postscript: Just opened the above letter to add another more recent occurrence. The fellow I nearly ran over in town yesterday turns out to be Vera's guardian, a well-mannered Russian named Serge Vassilovitch. About an hour ago he was admitted to my study. His smile, which is a ready one, reveals a double row of white, pointed teeth between lips as full and red as a painted woman's. There clung about him a strangely suggestive odor, most disagreeable to my nostrils; it was damp, musty, stale—it reminded me of the smells of the animal cages at the zoölogical gardens. Probably the heavy gray fur on his coat carried the odor. All in all, in spite of his really charming manners, his personality was not one that attracted; instead, it repelled me strongly, and I felt instinctive distrust of him.

He told me that my license number had served as a clew to my address, and declared that he had recognized his ward under her heavy veils, although how he could have done so is more than I can understand, for I would not know my own wife under the thick layers of chiffon Vera had swathed about her pretty face.

Vassilovitch took me into his confidence with regard to Vera, although I could see he wasn't very happy about shaking the family skeleton's bones in public. Poor Vera! Her story is tragic. Her father went insane and shot himself; her mother threw herself from a window to certain death under an insane impulse; Vera herself has been possessed, since her mother's death, with hallucinations so strange, so bizarre that her lack of mental poise could not be doubted for a moment by any one to whom she had told her story.

"Why, she believes," said he, with grieved accents, "that her nearest and dearest are persecuting her. She declares that I am her worst enemy—I, her natural protector!"

He asked me if she had told us her story, and seemed oddly contented—if I have observed correctly—when I replied that we could extract nothing from her in explanation of her extremely odd behavior. He shook his head sadly. "If she were to tell you her so-called story," he explained, "you would realize that she is mentally unbalanced."

As I have mentioned, Vassilovitch was a pleasant-mannered fellow, but I felt so uneasy in his presence that it seemed to me as if I couldn't bear being shut up with him alone, and I made an excuse to open the door into the front hall. Silly and womanish, if you will, but you know that what we call intuition may often be well founded, and I feel that Serge Vassilovitch does not possess a good influence. I therefore dissipated it as much as possible.

After his explanation I felt it only right that he should see Vera and that the girl should have the opportunity to give us her side of the story, which was certainly due to my wife and me, after our having taken the girl in, a complete stranger, as we had. Her guardian agreed strongly with me on this point, and said very reasonably that he felt sure, after she had told her story, that we would be only too glad to turn her over to his care again.

I called Myra to bring Vera, but my wife replied that she did not know where the girl was and that she had apparently left the house when she saw her guardian enter it. Here was a fine to-do! And Vassilovitch seemed terribly upset. He spread those red lips of his tightly against his sharp white teeth in a kind of threatening snarl, and actually demanded of Myra if she would give her word of honor that she didn't know where the young lady was. He left finally, but not without stating definitely that he would return in a day or two. Myra thought his words and his manner distinctly threatening. The menace was worse because of its very indefinableness.

Myra insists vehemently that Vera is not out of her head. "I tell you, Andy," she declares, "that the girl has had such a terrible nervous shock that she is afraid no one will believe her if she tells her experience."

Vera, it appears, had been hidden in the garret, and since Myra did not know her exact whereabouts she felt that she could conscientiously tell Vassilovitch that she didn't know where the girl was. Funny idea of truth women have! Vera insists upon remaining in the garret, where she can jump out of a window and die instantly at will, as she expresses it. Draw your own conclusions as to whether or not she intends to return to her guardian.

I am sadly disturbed, Tom. I simply cannot make head or tail of the affair. Myra says Vera is as sane as she is herself, and Vera weeps hysterically when asked for an explanation, crying that she will kill herself rather than fall into the hands of Serge Vassilovitch.

If you can't come down, write me your opinion Tom. Whether the girl is mentally deranged or no her guardian claims that she is not of age and that he can therefore take her to his home by force, if he can find her. I am persuaded that she would rather die than return with him. I am sending this special delivery. Hastily,   ANDREW.

Telegram from Doctor Connors to Doctor Greeley, late afternoon of the day the above letter was received.

Will be with you to-night without fail. Don't let Miss Andrevik out of your sight under any circumstances.   TOM.

Resumption of Doctor Connors' narrative.

I STUDIED the young girl carefully during dinner. All she said or did rang true. I felt convinced that she was as well poised mentally as any of us, but I sensed an atmosphere of nerve strain about her and saw the spirit of keen suffering looking at me out of her beautiful, sad eyes. However, in a case of this kind one can never make true judgment without extended observation, and I was sure that something would be said or done before the evening was over that would give me the key to the situation. Moreover, I had come to a conclusion as to the source of the trouble which I know you have already surmised.

We adjourned to the library, a small, cozy room, after dinner. Doctor Greeley turned on the electric fan, for Miss Andrevik insisted that all windows on the lower floor especially should be closed and fastened at night, and the evening was very close and sultry. We chatted lightly about nothing in particular, until I felt that the time had arrived for me to bring up the real occasion for my visit. I turned to Vera, and was about to touch on the subject lying nearest the hearts of us all when I distinctly heard—underneath the library window giving on the front porch —a singular whining, snuffling noise, as of some big animal nosing around.

Vera stiffened in her chair. I reached out instinctively and took her hand in mine; I was sitting near her. It was as cold as ice, poor child. Silence reigned in the room, while we listened intently.

We heard the noise of taloned feet, half padding and half clicking, across the boards of the porch flooring; the soft thud as the animal—whatever it was—sprang over the rail into the garden; and then a howl burst upon our startled ears that fairly lifted Vera from her chair. She pulled her hands from mine, rose to her feet as if impelled, and with a wail of terror threw herself upon the floor with her head in Mrs. Greeley's lap. As she hid her face she moaned: "It is he! It is he! Oh, don't let him take me away!"

Mrs. Greeley looked across at me half defiantly as she smoothed Vera's head with her motherly hands. The doctor looked at me with a wordless inquiry that demanded a reply. I gave it, knowing that at the same time I was giving courage to the poor tormented girl, struggling with the terrible memories of her horrible experiences.

"Miss Andrevik is no more out of her head than I am," I said aloud. "I am going to whisper four words into her ear, and they are so magical," I affirmed lightly, "that she will find courage to tell me the things hidden in her heart and which she has dared to disclose because she believed she would be thought insane if she told them."

How quickly the poor girl raised her white face to search my eyes for the help I promised! I made her sit once more in her easy-chair, and then, leaning over her, I whispered the four words into her eager ears. You know, dear master, what those words were. For a moment she sat rigid like one entranced; then the revulsion of feeling that swept over her bowed her, sobbing, while Mrs. Greeley almost glared at me in her fear that I had hurt the girl whom she had grown to love like a daughter.

"Oh, how can I ever thank you?" cried Vera. "Yes, now I will have courage to tell you, for I know you will understand. If you could only realize how I have doubted even my own eyes these awful days, Doctor Connors!"

Another long, quavering howl broke upon our ears. Mrs. Greeley turned to me with an explanation. "It's a big dog," said she. "I saw him come into our garden just about dusk this evening. He is a big, gray, shaggy fellow. He has been haunting our garden of late at night, and he has a most disagreeable howl. I don't know to whom he belongs, but I certainly wish they would tie the brute up at night," she ended a trifle angrily.

I exchanged glances with Miss Andrevik, whose eyes were eloquent with meaning, and answered her in kind. Then I told my friends the four words I had whispered into her ear and that had worked such a magic change in her whole attitude, loosening her tongue and removing her fear to tell her story. Of course it was only natural that Doctor Greeley should give me a look of penetrating and disturbed amazement; he thought my mind had given way. His wife contented herself with a look of simple inquiry.

"I see that neither of you understand my words," I smiled tranquilly. "I can explain later on. Just now I want to learn the details of Miss Andrevik's story, so that I may decide upon my course of action. Depend upon it, there is more here than appears on the surface."

Again our conversation was punctuated by that mournful, ominous cry from without. Vera shuddered, but without her former hysterical symptoms; she knew that she had found a protector who was able to guard her; her thankful eyes told me that.

"You may not have heard a cry like that before, Andy," I observed to Doctor Greeley. "But I have hunted all over the world, and, whether you believe it or not, that is no dog's howl; that is the howl of a wolf that you hear to-night, and a wolf of a very savage kind, too, if I am not mistaken. Miss Andrevik's story will undoubtedly throw much light upon the matter, although it may not only sorely try her courage in the telling, but will tax your credulity tremendously. Before she begins, I want to assure her that I can and will believe every word of her recital."

Once more I sought her glance, and her eloquent eyes thanked me. Then I requested the doctor to go the rounds of the house with me once more to make doubly sure that doors and windows were well secured. I turned lights on full in every room, merely stating that this was imperative, for I did not feel there was time for full explanations; it was borne in upon me that before day broke we would all have seen strange things. But as you had taught me, dear teacher, I made use of the Light, in its artificial form, to nullify the forces of evil which I knew were abroad.

Vera's story, as nearly in her own words as I can remember it, runs as follows.

Vera's narrative.

MY parents were Russian, and I was born in Russia. Coming under political suspicion because he had consorted with men not in his own class, my father was given to understand that he would be wise to leave the country. Converting into gold his large holdings, he took my mother and me and came to America. Serge Vassilovitch, one of the men with whom my father's association had brought him into disrepute, followed us in the course of three years. As they had both been students of the occult arts, in which my father had grown deeply interested, he was welcomed with open arms and given a home with us.

I was about ten years old. I spoke English fluently, having had an English governess, a good but stupid soul. I had never known anything but happiness in all my short life; always I had seen my mother laughing and my father good-humored. Therefore, I remember with what amazement I began to note my mother's face grow sad when she thought she was alone and with what dismay I discovered her more than once weeping. All this was after the arrival of Serge Vassilovitch.

My mother hid her trouble from my father, and it was not until long afterward that I learned the reason for her tears. Serge Vassilovitch loved my mother, and desired to take her away from my father, whom, however, she never ceased to love. He urged his guilty love upon her, only to be rebuffed repeatedly. Finally he swore that my mother should some day go to his arms whether she wanted to or not, and for some time he left her in peace. Then it was that my mother began to look sad and to weep in secret more than before, for my father fell so deeply under the spell of our evil genius that whatever Serge Vassilovitch proposed to him was as though foreordained. This condition of affairs went on for four years. I had grown to be tall and womanly and a companion to my dear mother, for I was seventeen years old when affairs reached a climax.

My father went so deeply into the study of the occult arts with Serge that it became his own and our undoing. Night after night they pored over unhallowed books of magic, and although I am sure Serge knew well what he was about my poor father was more weak and curious than he was wicked. He fell so entirely under the evil spell of that incarnation of Satan that he finally arrived at a place where he could not break with him, and actually believed everything Serge told him, even to entertaining suspicions of my dear mother. He drew up a will, as we discovered afterward, naming Serge my guardian and leaving in those hands all that should have been ours in trust; this shows you how deeply he believed in that vile man.

One day Serge's mad passion broke bounds; his years of restraint made him madder than ever before. He caught my mother to him, kissing her and holding her to him until she lost her strength and fell from him in an agony of shame at her weakness. She turned on him at last, then, telling him that another day should not pass before her husband should know how his friend had abused his confidence. Serge laughed at her scornfully. She told him that he must leave her roof at once, and he apparently acceded to her request. But although she little realized it, her momentary generosity in covering up the matter in her anxiety not to trouble my father became her undoing.

The following morning a child's body, mangled dreadfully as though by the teeth of a savage dog, was found in our grounds. We kept no dog, therefore suspicion did not attach to our household. But my father was closeted with Serge for hours after that discovery, and afterward he shut himself into his library, admitting no one. In the afternoon he came into my mother's room, where we sat embroidering, and kissed us both with a tender gravity which I felt portended something unusual. He laid a sealed envelope in my mother's lap, requesting her not to open it until circumstances seemed to demand it. Strange request! While my mother still sat staring with puzzled face at the envelope we heard a muffled shot. We ran down and pushed open the library door. Oh, my poor father! He had died, an innocent victim to that unmentionable devil whose evil influence had ruined all our lives. In his hand he still held the revolver with which he had hoped to purchase immunity for us from what he feared might be our fate.

After the agony of that experience was over my mother wanted to take me away, but our stern, implacable guardian refused to permit me to go, and my mother would not leave me, for she had already learned of Serge's further perfidy from my father's letter, and she dared not leave me with him.

My father's letter remained a sad secret with my mother during the year that we had together. During that year my poor mother was tortured in every conceivable manner imaginable by Serge Vassilovitch. Fearing both for me and for herself, she never left me alone for a moment, yet even in my presence that monster never desisted from inviting her to his arms with a cynicism that in itself was sufficiently revolting to a high-souled woman. It was toward the end of that first year of her widowhood that my mother learned the inner meaning of my father's letter—learned it from Serge's own lips.

My poor father had been the victim of a most vile plot, and had taken his own life in the belief that in so doing he was expiating his unconscious crime. Under Serge Vassilovitch's spell, he had been led to believe that, owing to the magic arts they had practiced together, the power of metamorphosis into the form of a wolf had been bestowed upon him by certain evil powers. Serge had himself killed the child, and had shown the mangled body to my father, declaring that in the form of a wolf my poor parent had destroyed and torn the innocent. Imagine the consternation and horror of a high-minded man who had unwisely permitted himself to dabble in magic arts that had brought him to such a pass. His remorse was terrible. He felt that, having unconsciously committed one such crime, he might in future commit others. He believed there was but one way out and like a true and noble gentleman he took that way, no even giving his beloved wife an opportunity to dissuade him.

The awful story of his supposed crime formed the contents of his letter to my mother. Oh, if he had only come to her instead of taking that final step! My mother knew that he had laid by her side all that night. She taxed Serge, who laughed fiendishly, and admitted that he had lied to my father, thus forcing him to take his own life.

"Clearing the way very thoughtfully for his successor," said he sardonically.

Struck to the heart by the horror of the revelation, my mother attempted to flee with me, but Serge had given out that she was mentally unbalanced; we were stopped and forced to return. With scorn and loathing in her heart, she rebuffed his suit daily. But one afternoon, as I sat with my mother, embroidering, I felt his eyes upon me strangely. He was regarding me with such an expression that I suddenly feared him horribly, sprang up with a cry, and rushed to my mother's side. She caught me to her with a gasp of such anguish that it seems as if I could hear it now.

"Was not one victim enough for you?" she asked.

"Well," he returned with insolent indifference, "I was just wondering if, after all, I ought not to prefer the bud to the blossom."

There was a long pause. Then my mother said in a strange, hard voice: "You have won. Give me this one night in peace." And she still held me to her, while her labored breath shook her entire body.

Serge went slowly away with a backward smile, hatefully exposing his sharp white teeth with an air of knowing triumph.

My mother locked the door. She barred the window. Then she sat down, pulled me down beside her, and whispered the whole awful truth to me. I listened, my brain whirling, for it appeared to me that what they said must be true, and that my mother's mind had been injured by my father's tragic death.

Little by little, however, convinced by her deadly seriousness, by my father's letter, and by my own emotions of fear and horror when in the presence of my guardian, I began to credit her. I saw but one thing to do, and that was to attempt escape, even if we died in the attempt. My mother was firm in her intention to kill herself rather than fall into those evil hands, and, while she said nothing to me, I knew she would not leave me behind her. We whispered our plans to escape that very night. With youth's optimism I knew I could find something to do that would support my mother and myself. And in spite of her anxiety, my mother smiled her lovely smiles at me again for the first time in months.

When the house was sleeping soundly we crept out on the porch roof, and my mother slipped down a pillar to the ground, turning to hold out her arms to me. I was halfway down the roof when my mother's voice rang out in an agony of fear and horror.

"Vera, Vera, go back! Save yourself! The revolver! My God, it is the wolf of the steppes!"

As she cried out to me I saw a huge shape as of some great shaggy beast spring upon her from the darkness, bearing her to the ground. Something raised its head from where she lay, her cries silenced forever, and I roused myself from my apathy of deadly fear to scramble back into my window, away from the horror of those terrible fiery eyes, red and evil, that looked leering upon me from over my unfortunate mother's dead body. My senses were failing me, but I managed to get back into the room, and had hardly closed and fastened the shutter before I heard the thud of a heavy body upon the porch roof.

My mother's words echoed in my dizzy brain: "Save yourself, Vera! The revolver——" I looked about me hastily in the dim candlelight. On my mother's dressing table I saw a revolver, and I caught it up, crying out to the Thing that waited without: "If you try to break in here, I shall shoot you. I am armed."

The Thing sniffed around the window frame for a few moments, then sprang to the ground. I felt my senses leaving me, and I fell back on my mother's bed, unconscious.

With morning came voices, shrieks, feet running here and there, knockings on my door. I dared not open; I was terribly afraid of everything and everybody in that awful house. I heard my guardian's exclamations of horror at the discovery of my mother's mangled body, and it seemed to me as if I could not live through those moments of intense suffering. How I got through the day without losing my mind I do not know; I do remember that I lost myself in periods of unconsciousness several times.

Toward evening came the voice of my guardian at the door, stern and commanding. "Open at once, foolish girl!" he demanded.

I kept silence.

"If you do not open to me at once, Vera, I shall be obliged to break in the door."

"If you try to come in," I replied with desperate bravado, "I have a bullet ready for you."

He laughed with cold scorn. "Hunger will drive you out soon enough," he commented aloud. "But it will be better for you in the end to open now than later."

I felt that his words hid a mystery too terrible for explanation. But I remained firm. I was convinced that between Serge and the wolf of the steppes there was some evil connection.

After a while he seemed to have gone away, for I heard no sound. But at last came a sniffing around the cracks of the door and the scratching of sharp claws on the panels. He had sent the Thing that had killed my mother! Oh, how pitiless he was! I had heard of the wolf of the steppes, but had believed it only a superstition, yet my intuition told me that that which waited without was not a dog.

I cried out to it to go away, and finally it went, only to come to my window, whining and snarling there and scratching at the shutters.

"Go away!" I called again, cold fear clutching at my heart. "If anything tries to come in at this window I shall shoot on sight."

The howlings died away. Ominous silence ensued. I heard only the soft thud as the beast landed on the ground before the porch. You may well imagine what a night I passed, knowing that perhaps the Thing waited beneath my window. Just as morning broke I peered through a chink in the shutter and saw it for the first time. It was a great, gray, shaggy wolf; it bounded out of the bushes and stood, with slavering jaws, looking up at my window with its evil, red-rimmed eyes. It seemed to me that those eyes could penetrate the slats of the shutters and could see me watching from behind them. It raised its head and gave a long, dreadful howl.

Then, as I looked, I thought my eyes must be deceiving me, for it stood upright like a man. As the light grew stronger from the rising sun, the shaggy coat seemed to turn into civilized garments, and there, suddenly, where the wolf had stood, was my guardian, gazing up at my window with venomous ugliness upon his wicked face. This time I did not lose my senses, for I realized with what I had to deal. All the old nursery tales told me of the wolf of the steppes when I was a little girl in Russia came to my mind again. I knew that the werewolf was discredited in America and that if I were to claim such a thing about my guardian I would not be believed, and might even be called insane, as my mother was. There was but one thing to be done; I must escape, even at the cost of my life.

That afternoon I saw Serge go on horseback down the road, and seized the favorable opportunity, only to be disillusioned. My governess, with pity in her eyes, turned me back, calling one of the servants to her aid. I realized that I was being guarded as would be a mad creature, so I went back, locking myself into my room. I was weak from want of food, but dared not open the door again, lest my guardian should return. Late afternoon brought him to my door again.

I had by then planned everything. I told him that if he would permit me to have ten minutes alone after the sun set I would unlock the door then. I heard him laugh quietly to himself, and I knew what his thoughts were; he did not know that I knew him for what he was; he thought I was prepared to receive an odious lover, and undoubtedly he was already thinking of how he would mangle my body with his metamorphosed talons and his sharp white teeth!

He told me that as an earnest of my good intentions I must surrender the revolver. This I had not expected, but I rose equal to the occasion.

"I dare not open the door to you now," I replied. "But I will throw it out of the window."

"Very well, Vera," assented my guardian. I heard his footsteps retiring down the hall, and knew he would go outside to retrieve the weapon, which I had no intention of giving up.

I took a silver-mounted hairbrush from my mother's dressing table, opened the window cautiously, and when I heard his steps on the graveled path below I threw the brush with all my force as far as I could into the bushes. He ran to get it. And then I unlocked my door, flew down the stairs, out of the front door, and down the path, thanking God that this time no one had appeared to stop me and putting my trust in Him that there would be some one outside who could save me from the horrible fate that might otherwise await me, unless I took the sad alternative of self-death.

Hardly was I out of sight of the house before I heard a long and dreadful howl of fury. I knew that the wolf of the steppes had found my door open and the room empty. Fear seemed to hold my feet to the ground. I clutched at my revolver, giving myself up as lost, when I heard Doctor Greeley's automobile coming down the road. You know the rest of the story.

Resumption of Doctor Connors' narrative.

THE poor girl hardly dared meet her friends' eyes while telling the almost unbelievable tale, but upon finishing she turned imploringly to Mrs. Greeley, who half avoided her eyes and looked inquiringly at me. I replied to her questioning look with a glance of assurance, and turned to Vera.

"My dear Miss Andrevik, there is every reason for me to believe your story, since I have been a witness of just such a metamorphosis in Persia. Lycanthropy is on the wane, because the waste places of the world—forgathering places for spiritual forces of good and evil—are becoming peopled, and with added population such manifestations become more and more unusual. You may rest assured that I do not think you insane, and until I can explain the matter more fully to your friends they must take my word for it that you are unusually well-poised mentally, else you could never have come through such a terrible experience unscathed."

Vera's next thought was that, as she was a minor, her guardian would be able to claim her legally. To this I replied that there was but one thing to do, and that was to remove such a menace forever from the world. That I was determined to do this you can well understand; the only difficulty in the way was that if I shot the wolf the dead man would remain on our hands, according to the laws of lycanthropic metamorphosis, and I really did not like to think of hunting up Serge Vassilovitch and shooting him down in cold blood—murderer though he was—in bright daylight, in order to assure his transformation into a wolf, which alone would save me from a charge of manslaughter. The only way out of the dilemma was to kill the wolf and then rely upon a certain formula which you taught me to use under special conditions to transform into the wolf form permanently the slain Serge Vassilovitch. The authorities certainly might wonder at a wolf's being at large in the town, but they could not object to its being killed, especially if it had attacked any of us, as it would be certain to do if given sufficient opportunity. My object was to kill it before it could do any damage, either to any of us or to outsiders.

I instructed Doctor and Mrs. Greeley not to let Vera out of their sight, and to keep all their doors scrupulously secured, especially at night. I bade Vera retire and sleep sweetly, secure in the knowledge that one who understood her problem was watching over her safety. When Mrs. Greeley went upstairs with the girl my friend turned to me, and with severe gravity demanded an explanation of my "idiotic rigmarole." I gave it; dear master, I gave it very fully and completely. When the sun's rays brought us respite from our guard I was still explaining to my very skeptical friend. I promised him a sight of the metamorphosis, which he admitted would be a convincing proof of my "theories." He refused to believe that I could have seen just such a transformation with my own very good eyes.

For three days we kept closely to the house, and

on the evening of the third day I saw the wolf of the steppes slipping behind a clump of bushes in the garden, and felt convinced that that night would see the last act played out. I had provided myself with the necessary articles, and awaited with impatience for the darkness to fold down upon us. I had cleared all movables out of the library, so that there would be plenty of free space. I stationed Doctor Greeley behind one of the French windows with a revolver, and I arranged a morris chair at the farther end of the room, behind which I crouched. The window was left unfastened, so that, at a light touch from without, it would swing inward.

We had planned that when the wolf entered, as it undoubtedly would, unless it were warier than I gave it credit for being, Doctor Greeley would immediately close the window behind it, turning on the light at the same time. If the creature turned and saw him, he was to shoot; otherwise, I would get a splendid opportunity from my ambush to finish the night terror of Russia. Each of us was also armed with a hunting knife, in case we came into close contact with the beast.

All happened as we had planned. We had hardly been in place fifteen minutes before we heard the padding and scraping of the taloned claws on the porch flooring, and a moment later a sniffing at the window, which, at the touch, swung slowly open. The moon had risen over the treetops, and her soft light poured into the room, rendering other light unnecessary. I saw the animal hesitate on the threshold for a moment; then it came into the room with a single bound, and sprang across to the inside door opening into the hall.

For an instant my heart stood still with apprehension. Had we forgotten to close that inner door in our anxiety to plan for the entrance of the wolf? No, the beast paused again before that closed door, and then began to pace back to the window. My friend closed it quickly, but in so doing stood against the moonlight in full view of the werewolf. I rose from behind my ambush and took quick aim, firing almost simultaneously with Doctor Greeley. Which of our shots took fatal effect I do not know to this day, since both were in vital spots. The great gray beast lifted itself into the air with a single convulsive movement, while a terrible howl of pain and fury burst from it. Doctor Greeley sprang to one side just in the nick of time, for the falling werewolf, with its dying effort, struck and snapped at the place where my friend had been standing, then rolled back upon the floor, twitching with a dying spasm.

I turned on the light, and my friend and I drew cautiously near to the dead animal. Then I turned triumphantly to him, I must confess, and wordlessly pointed to what lay on the library floor. Clad in his gray, fur-trimmed overcoat, now stained with red, Serge Vassilovitch lay with staring, furious garnet eyes, quite motionless.

Doctor Greeley looked as though he could not credit his own eyes, and then turned to me incredulously. "I could have sworn it was a wolf," said he slowly, horror-stricken.

I laughed. "In a short time you will see, with your own eyes, the transformation of this dead murderer into the werewolf form," I promised.

"Seeing's believing," he retorted.

The shots had brought both women down into the hall, and we heard their voices outside the door calling to us. I opened the door a trifle to say that all was well and the wolf dead. Then I added that they would do well to retire to an upstairs room for a while, and that they were not to come down under any circumstances. While Mrs. Greeley did not realize the gravity of this injunction, I saw that Vera Andrevik understood what I was about to do, for her eyes opened, startled, she drew Mrs. Greeley from the room, closed the door, and I heard their voices as they mounted the stairs to seek Vera's room, where I knew she would hold Mrs. Greeley until I had finished my incantation.

I closed door and windows. Then I carried out the instructions that you gave me, dear master, inclosing in one circle the dead murderer and in another double circle my friend and myself. I set the brazier in position, poured the prepared powder upon the glowing charcoal, and called thrice upon the Spirit of Evil. The first time such a deadly silence fell upon us that it struck cold to the palpitating heart; the second time a rushing wind came suddenly from nowhere and seemed to center itself upon the house, shaking it as with an earthquake shock; the third time—oh, dear master and teacher, it is well that you taught me to school my soul against the emotion of fear! When I felt the approach of the essence of wickedness materialized I feared for my friend, and made him kneel within the inner circle, bowing his head upon his clasped arms. Then I braced myself physically and lifted my head high to meet whatever was to come. It was more terrible than I had imagined!

From out the now dense darkness gathered unseen forces that I felt were pushing and pulling against the magic circle of protection. I knew that an instant's weakness on my part would give them entrance. I dared not rely upon my own strength entirely, and from the depths of my soul I sent out a cry to Adonai for courage and endurance. And it came—it came! But the Evil grew ever stronger and stronger, and I realized that I must use every ounce of my will to keep fear from my heart that the magic circle might not break, weakened by my weakness. I kept my eyes fixed upon the dead that lay within the farther circle.

The moon no longer shone in at the windows but there was a light that seemed to shine from where I stood and my friend knelt. Also the light from the brazier threw flickering tongues of brightness over the room now and then. When the moment came that I knew I could bear it no longer I called with a loud voice upon the Evil that lurked in the shade about us.

"In the name of Adonai, I have summoned you, powerful Spirit of Evil, because ye dare not refuse obedience to the supreme power. In the same Ineffable Name I call upon you thrice to break the spell that permits this dead that was a man to remain man after death. Beast he became of choice, and beast he must remain. In the name of Adonai, I admonish you, give him not the form of man again! In the name of Adonai, I command you, keep him ever in the form of that beast which he chose to assume!

In the name of Adonai, aid him not again, alive or dead! And now, begone!"

As I called upon the name of the Mighty One I felt new life and courage and power flowing into my veins, and I knew that I was speaking with authority.

I looked upon the dead that lay near by, and saw that the change had begun, so I touched my friend upon the shoulder. He lifted his head cautiously; his face was quite gray and drawn, for he had felt the spiritual influence of that Evil near us, and he had not been prepared, like myself, to resist and defeat it. His eyes fell upon the other circle, and in the soft light of the brazier I saw them dilate with incredulous astonishment.

Together we saw the metamorphosis of what had been Serge Vassilovitch into the wolf of the steppes, in which form that base spirit must remain imprisoned for the allotted space. My friend is convinced now that my "theories" are not groundless!

As the last of the transformation took place I felt a glad lightening of my spirits, and realized that the Evil about us, which I had called to undo its work, was about to depart. The rushing of a mighty wind again whirled about the house and departed whence it came, and, as it went, the moon's light broke forth from behind the clouds that had swathed it and burst out in full splendor, throwing into relief the body of the great gray wolf that lay within the farther circle. I stepped from the circle and turned on light.

My friend met my smiling gaze with a look that impressed me with the awe he yet felt after our experience. "My dear Tom," he finally said, "I agree with *Hamlet* most sincerely and fully. There *are* stranger things than we know of. Let it go at that, old man."

We both laughed, for the ordeal was over, and with its passing came a revulsion of spirit that was welcome.

The body of the dead wolf was turned over to the authorities the following day. I suggested that possibly it had escaped from some traveling menagerie, and my explanation was accepted on the face of it.

Miss Andrevik has been formally adopted by my friends, the Greeleys, and her father's fortune finally turned over to her in the unexplainable absence of her guardian, Serge Vassilovitch. She has become as light-hearted as could be expected of a girl who had passed through such a gruesome and grueling experience. I may add that her extreme youth and the love she now finds we all have for her may have had something to do with helping her to regain her girlish happiness once so horribly threatened.

There is no more to relate at this moment, master, save that I hope some day to bring Vera with me to receive your blessing. As yet I have not spoken to her, but our eyes have said much that our lips do not yet feel licensed to speak.

Greetings, O Amdi Rubdah, from your pupil,
THOMAS CONNORS.

Our Idea

Did you ever stop to consider that the weird, fantastic story is essentially fundamental in truth and plausibility? In every issue of the large newspapers you strike incidents, experiences, that outrival the wildest fancies of Jules Verne. If this were not true, why is it that Poe plays such an important part in world literature? The fact is that unseen things are every bit as interesting as the seen. The trouble is that many stories of this kind are poorly done. This will explain why we are so anxious to print only the best. We receive many manuscripts, but we are not going to put them out unless they come up to the highest standard.

Ivory Hunters
By Will Gage Carey

IT was through a mutual friend in a quiet café just off Kearney Street that I made the acquaintance of Captain Boyer.

"What's your business?" he asked bluntly, after the conventional remarks anent our introduction.

"Well, cap'n," I answered, "before going into that permit me to put a question or two to you."

"Go ahead."

"You're a seafaring man?" I began.

"Yes."

"And make extended ocean voyages from time to time?"

"Yes; in the finest little craft afloat—the *Frisco Maid*."

"And your purpose in making these voyages——"

"Hunting ivory."

I reached over and clasped his huge hand again. "Shake once more, cap'n," I said. "I'm in a similar line myself. I, too, am an ivory hunter."

"No!"

"Yes."

He stroked his chin thoughtfully. "Strange," he observed at length. "I've never run across you before. What's your route? Where do you go for ivory?"

"Oh, I've been most all over this country——"

"'*This*' country?" he broke in wonderingly.

"Why, yes."

"Ever been down among the South Sea Islands?"

"No; but I believe there is a chance to pick up ne good stuff down that way. What I want right now, however, is to take a little jaunt far up into the Arctic Sea——"

"The *Frisco Maid* sails for there in three days."

This was interesting news to me; I resumed our discussion with animation. "It's this way with me, cap'n," I said. "I'm an ivory hunter all right—and a mighty particular one at that. I don't buy up all the goods I'm offered, see? But when I see what I want I'm able and ready to pay the price. Now, if you're bound for the Far North, take me with you; not to share in the profits of the voyage, but to pick out just what I want to buy. I'll interfere in no manner with your own transactions. Let me pay you a stipulated price to take me along, that price to include the charges on my own particular cargo back."

He didn't seem to take to the idea much at first; but after thinking it over for a time he named a price which suited me well enough. Three days later I sailed out through the Golden Gate, bound for the Far, Far North, aboard the trim little *Frisco Maid*.

Now, I can say this for Captain Boyer: Our business transaction completed, he asked me no more questions concerning either myself or my manner of conducting my work as an ivory hunter; not but what there was much he did not fully understand in this connection, but he was not the kind to meddle in another's affairs. And I resolved not to see too much of what was going on in connection with his own private business negotiations, which was fair enough.

It was early summer; the voyage up the coast was delightful. Our ship was small, but stanch—as good as any in the trade. Besides full sail equipment, she carried twin Diesel engines, and we made good speed in either wind or calm. We had a full crew, including a ship's surgeon, electrician, gunners, hunters, skinners. Grub was plentiful, with occasional rations of something strengthening by way of drink to go with our salt pork and sea biscuit. Our cap'n, while much of a crab at times, knew his business to a fare-ye-well; the ship's officers were rather a decent lot, and, all things considered, we of the *Frisco Maid* looked forward to a fair and prosperous voyage.

Captain Boyer was a man of good education, and when so inclined was an entertaining conversationalist. During one of the few intervals in which we discussed business I asked him just where he expected to obtain his supply of ivory. "From the tusks of walrus," he answered.

"And the grade?"

"Not up to that of elephant tusks, of course," he answered, "but still of good commercial quality. The upper canines of the walrus consist of a body of dentine invested with cementum; they are oval in section, solid, and their axis is made up of secondary dentine far larger in amount than in the hippopotamus, and makes up a considerable portion of the whole tooth. While rather nodular in appearance when cut and polished, it is of dense and tolerably uniform consistence; then, too, there is the spirally twisted tusk of the norwhal, of slightly less commercial value——"

"Any other source of revenue for you on this trip?" I asked innocently enough.

He sized me up searchingly before replying; then, seemingly satisfied, he answered: "Understand me, Mr. Moggs, we are not poachers; we are out mainly for tusks, though I will say that we have decided that in case we come across any island which seems *over-crowded* to the point of discomfort with seals—well, we *might* take on a few skins in such a case, just as an act of human kindness. I think you understand the feelings which would prompt anything of this kind, Mr. Moggs?"

"I'm sure I do," I answered.

That night, alone in my bunk, I went over our conversation again in detail, trying to determine just what I was up against and what would be my chance of getting out again without encountering serious trouble. There was no question in my mind now about the purpose of the little *Frisco Maid* in arctic waters; I was aboard a poacher—that much was certain. The risk was great; the penalty would be severe if we were caught, and the fact that I was an innocent party aboard the seal poacher might be an extremely difficult matter to prove.

Far, far to the north we sailed, each day bringing new adventures, some new crisis to meet in storms, fogs, and the constant threatenings of gigantic icebergs. We came to an island. Small and rugged it was, and so crowded with flappy seals that they kept pushing each other off into the water. The captain stood at the rail of the poop deck, glass in hand. Then he raised it and gazed long and longingly at the restless, uncomfortable seals forever pushing each other off over the slippery brink; then he turned to me with the observation: "Poor—poor things; we must do something for them, Mr. Moggs, and at once!"

We stayed a week at that little island. The seething mass of seals became perceptibly thinner; the hold of the *Frisco Maid* settled deeper into the water. Then one day we saw the smoke from a distant funnel upon the horizon. We left in all haste, lest the approaching U. S. revenue cutter put a wholly wrong interpretation upon our presence in the vicinity. For weeks and weeks we sailed straight north then. It was hardly the Old Man's preconceived idea to go *quite* so far north, but it seems that the revenue cutter was going north, too; they kept in so closely behind us we were forced to the belief at times that we were being chased.

Now we were very far to the north; it seemed to me away into a different realm. The sea itself had a peculiar roll and was of a strange, copper color. The sky, for the most part, was a drab gray, but during the few hours each day that the sun shone it turned to an emerald shade, with a magenta fringe. Strikingly beautiful, but uncanny; very uncanny.

A little later we steered into a great bank of gray fog; then something got wrong with the rudder. We couldn't keep to our course, but were swept along by ocean currents in a northeasterly direction. Finally we came out from the fog bank, but we had lost our bearings, which was bad for us; but we'd lost all track of the revenue cutter, and that was something to be thankful for. The sun came out. Around us were icebergs, mountain high, glittering like molten silver. We were at mercy of the current, but it guided us in and out through the maze of towering peaks in a way which seemed almost supernatural. Darkness came on again, and of a sudden we felt a great shock against our bow which jarred every timber in the ship. We had been swept ashore by the current, upon—so we learned later—a great island of ice about a quarter of a league from a bleak promontory which projected from a mainland still more frigid, desolate, and wind-swept.

Just at our leeward was a great ledge of ice we could nearly reach out and touch from the ship's rail, and when the sun again shone forth there appeared along this ledge a throng of natives, who perched up there on the crest, watching us with listless eyes, side by side, like so many fat, stuffed birds. They were a strange race of people, with blue orbs, yellow hair, and features regular enough, save that their eyes seemed, for the most part, to be set slightly on the bias.

There they sat, blinking down at us, without a sound or move, as though it was quite a regular thing to have a ship beached upon their shore and that the whole affair had been arranged and staged for their entertainment and amusement. Right in the center of the line was the chief—bigger than the others and dressed in finer furs. His little beady eyes took in every detail of what was going on aboard the ship. He seemed kindly disposed and reasonably intelligent, despite the depressing apathy of his fat followers. All our efforts failing to get the vessel off the strand proving futile, we thought best to try to get into some sort of communication with our silent audience. The Old Man was the first to make the attempt. We awaited results anxiously.

Going up close to the rail, he called out in Swedish: *"Hur ai du i dag!"*

The chief turned his head on one side and looked down at him like an owl, but he never batted an eye. Then the first mate—a Pole—tried his hand at making conversation. *"Jak sie pan masz!"* he called up expectantly. The chief scratched his ear and sort of grinned; then the ship's surgeon got in with: *"Pongo Tomale, señor?"*

At this the big chief stood up, yawned, bit off a chew of navy plug, and drawled out: "You poor nuts —can't you talk United States?"

II.

TWO minutes later we were prisoners. While those blonds on the bluff were holding our attention in front, another bigger squad had sneaked out to sea in boats, circled back, climbed up over our stern, and had us roped hand and foot before we had a chance to put up anything like a fight. Then, as though we were so many mummies, they shouldered us—fifteen in all—took us in their boats to the mainland, then set off over the ice for their village; but they never offered to touch anything else aboard the *Frisco Maid.*

We came in sight of a large cluster of snow and ice houses at length, some of considerable size and looking like great inverted bowls. The merry villagers came trooping out to meet us. Such a mob —all talking and laughing at once! Behind the men came the women and girls. Some damsels! They wore their hair in long yellow braids down their backs, and while they didn't do much talking—vocally—using their big lustrous blue eyes they began a discourse with our husky young men both animated and ardent; a universal language known and understood the world over, in every realm and clime.

The men of this strange land, however, soon ceased their boisterous shouts and clamor; it was evident that, to them, there was no foolishness about this business. And from their manner and stern, set faces we sensed the fact that our plight was not only one of discomfort, but actually perilous as well.

They took us directly to a great council hall built of huge ice blocks. Here they sat us down and removed our thongs. The big chief arose and began a neat little speech. I tell you, it made us mighty fidgety, sitting there in that great, glittering dome, with those big blond wallopers giving us "the once over" with critical and exacting eyes—not saying a word, understand; just sort of appraising and estimating.

In his speech, the chief—Oo-gloo, he said his name was—got right down to cases, and I must say that he was as nice about it as existing conditions would permit. He commenced by stating that desperate conditions necessitated desperate measures; that he and his tribe thought best to make captives of us for the reason that they were facing—that very moment— actual starvation!

I have spoken of the natives looking fat and sleek —and so they were; but to attain such condition they had consumed nearly the entire food supply of the village. You would have thought that when they saw themselves running short of rations they would have eased up a bit on the big eats, but it seems that wasn't their style. While food lasted they lived high, trusting in a kind Providence to see them safely through. They regarded *us* as the answer of kind Providence for their trusting faith!

As I say, Chief Oo-gloo was delicacy itself in dealing with the situation. He went on to state that everything depended now upon the east wind; should the wind turn to that quarter, the ice pack which obstructed their fishing grounds would be swept away; then the tribe could venture forth and catch sea food in abundance. Also, with the changing of the wind to the east, great herds of caribou and musk oxen would appear. That would mean good times and feasting for all—ourselves included. The wind might change to the east at any moment; it was about a hundred-to-one shot, however, that it would *not* change any time soon—perhaps not for many long, dreary, hungry months!

Facing as they did this crisis, the Peroxides—as we named them—knowing not just what to expect, but realizing that they must eat, had made us captives pro tem, so to speak. We were to be what you might term a reserve fund, to be used solely as a last resort, as Chief Oo-gloo expressed it. Of course it looked bad for us—mere pawns and puppets of a capricious wind; but it must be admitted that Oo-gloo brought our attention to the matter with a degree of finesse and a considerate choice of words and clustering of phrases which made us hope for the best even while inwardly expecting the worse.

Furthermore, he went on to say that while food lasted—which could not be for long unless the wind changed—we were to be his guests and share alike with his people the scant supply of rations; we were to have the freedom of the community, and were not to be looked upon as prisoners—at least while the hunger of all could be appeased—all of which seemed highly satisfactory to those giggling blond girls and the heedless young men of our own party, who now lost no time in getting acquainted. Wonderful, wonderful race, those Peroxides, and wonderful, even now, to think back upon those days and nights of innocent amusement and revelry—riotous moments of mirth, music, and dancing, even with the mockery of a probable terrible fate staring at us from around the corner of a fast-emptying larder!

An intimation of approaching calamity came like a bolt from a clear sky, and it came in this manner: "Stewie"—our ship's cook—was short, fat and plump, with rosy cheeks and a tender manner. It became apparent to us that the natives had begun paying him marked attention. The most sumptuous ice house was his for quarters, his the brightest fire, his couch of the softest reindeer skins; also, he ate plenteously, while many of us were forced to scrimp. At first he was inclined to feel rather chesty over this apparent favoritism; then he began to get wise. Gradually it oozed down through his dome that the Peroxides had thus singled him out with some dark, sinister, ulterior purpose in mind.

He took the matter up, the first chance he got, with the Old Man. "Cap'n," he began dolefully, "friendship an' kindness are all right—up to a certain point——"

"Well, Stewie?"

"——but it strikes me these dog-gone Peroxides are too bloomin' kind an' friendly. It sort of seems to me these hungry boobs are framin' something on me. I think they—that is, I have a sort of sneakin' idea that——"

"Don't say it, Stewie!" broke in the captain. "I know just what you mean; I have the same suspicions as you yourself entertain. It looks bad. But what are we to do, ol' scout? We are stranded hard and fast. Even should we manage to escape from the Peroxides, we could not get the ship afloat without the aid of the whole tribe. We've got to use finesse, Stewie—great gobs of it! I'll have another confab with Chief Oo-gloo at once; I hope to be able to come and tell you soon that our secret fears in your behalf are without just cause and foundation."

The captain sought out Chief Oo-gloo at once, and, during the interview which followed, four large Peroxide warriors broke in upon poor Stewie and carried him away to a sort of fortress, where he had been ordered to be kept in solitary confinement pending such conditions and results as the next week or so might bring forth.

I don't know just what passed between the captain and Oo-gloo, but when the Old Man came out he was looking mighty glum, and he ordered that food supplies from the ship be carried into the village at once. Can goods, salt pork, sea biscuit—it was all a great treat for the natives; but we knew this couldn't go on for long. The source of supply was by no means inexhaustible, and when gone——

It was Oscar, the ship's surgeon, who led us back from the darkened depths of despondency to which we older heads had been plunged up into the regions of hope once more. One day, in snooping around his ice house, he came across a crude sort of baseball, with a walrus-hide cover. He took it at once to the crafty old ruler of the Peroxides. "Chief," he said, "what's this—a baseball?"

"Yes; you're right," Oo-gloo replied importantly.

"What! You mean to tell me, chief, you all play baseball up here?"

The chief's tone became patronizing: "*Do* we? Well, well! *Do* we?"

"Yes," continued the surgeon; "I ask—do you?"

Now no chief ever lived—anywhere—civilized or uncivilized, who didn't have some hobby, and the bigger they are the harder they fall for it. Oscar surmised he had tumbled next to the pet weakness of Chief Oo-gloo of the Peroxide clan; he determined to push this vantage point for all it was worth, and his alert mind was already working out a plan.

"We have," the chief resumed loftily, "a baseball team in this village that has trimmed everything north of parallel 79 to a fragmentary frazzle."

"Ah, indeed!"

"Oh, yes, indeed; that's just what we have. In our league our team is known as the 'Musk Oxen.'"

"It *must* be a strong team," observed the surgeon.

"Strong hardly does it justice," continued Oo-gloo, Oscar's remark going over his head. "I presume you didn't know we finished first in the Aurora Borealis League last season?"

"*Is* that right?"

"You bet that's right!"

"Well, well; that's strange."

"What's strange?"

"Why, we, too—among the crew and officers of the *Frisco Maid*—have a crackerjack ball team. I dare say, ours is the very best team that ever struck this neck of the woods——"

"Oh, I guess not *the* best!" broke in the chief with asperity. "I guess not hardly the best——"

"I said 'best,'" Oscar spoke up heatedly, "and that goes!"

Oo-gloo was getting furious, just as the wily surgeon hoped he would do. "Why, man, my Musks could take on your bunch of bushes, I have no hesitancy in saying, and make them look like a team of cripples. Say, you make me laugh! Now, I don't want to brag——"

"Oh, certainly not!"

"But you're sure in wrong if you think you've got any team that would show against the Musks——"

"I'll just call that!" Oscar came back at him strong. "In behalf of my Seals, I challenge you to a game this coming Saturday; I challenge you right now——"

"You're on!"

Then the surgeon got down to the real issue he had in mind. "One thing, chief, I must demand here and now."

"What do you demand?"

"The immediate release of Stewie, our cook."

"What has Stewie to do with a match game between the Musks and the Seals?"

"Everything."

"I don't get you."

For an instant only the surgeon was at a loss; then he answered: "Stewie is positively the one man among us who can handle the Seals. He is manager and trainer. If this proposed game is to take place, Stewie must be given his liberty at once and get to work on his team."

The chief frowned.

"There is absolutely no other way," added the surgeon in tones of finality.

"Well, I'll have him turned loose then," agreed Oo-gloo reluctantly, "for the time being; it is not long until Saturday, anyhow."

Encouraged by the results attained, Oscar pressed his point still further. "Another thing, Chief Oo-gloo——"

"Well, well—what now?"

"If the Seals win——"

"They won't!"

"But in case they *do* triumph over your Musks you must give me your sacred word of promise that you will have your people assist us in getting our ship afloat again, and that we may be allowed to depart in peace."

"Impossible; I tell you your departure depends solely upon a return of the east wind——"

"If defeated, we'll leave Stewie behind—after you have assisted us in getting the *Frisco Maid* afloat!" Oscar added in desperation. "You agree to this, and you'll see the grandest game of baseball you ever beheld."

Chief Oo-gloo pondered it over. Finally he extended his grimy hand. "It's a bargain," he said heartily. "You're a hard man to make terms with, but I'll let nothing stand in the way of seeing my Musks trounce those slippery Seals of yours to a fragmentary frazzle!" Then he added half pityingly: "With my strong Musk Oxen out there on the diamond—say, it almost seems a shame to take the money! Honestly now—just what odds should the betting take next Saturday?"

"Dollars to a *scent!*" Oscar shouted back as he hurried away to demand the freedom of Stewie, the rosy-cheeked cook.

III.

I T may seem strange that the chief, having us so completely in his power, would talk terms at all. But Oo-gloo was a true sport; he had his heart set on seeing his favorites mix with a team worthy of meeting his doughty champs of the Borealis League. Then, too—though we were virtually captives—he was inclined to give us a fair fighting chance. I had seen enough of the chief to believe him absolutely on the square; that he would live up to any agreement he made to the very letter, cost him what it might. Now, if we could only win from his Musks, we would be well out of a mess of trouble. Could we win!

Again, it might seem rather peculiar that the surgeon would agree, under any circumstances, to leave poor Stewie behind. Well, be assured he never would have done so had he not felt absolute faith that our team would have little trouble to down these Peroxide athletes, and our desperate situation seemed to necessitate taking this desperate chance.

The interview between the chief and the surgeon took place in the former's house, with only a few of us present; but with the agreements made and plans all formulated we went over to the counsel hall, where Oo-gloo called together his people and the balance of the ship's crew and told them of the great game scheduled for the coming Saturday. The Old Man—when he heard the terms upon which the challenge was made and accepted—was for backing out; but the members of the ball team talked him into believing it safe enough and that Stewie stood in no danger whatever of being left behind. Formal acceptance was then agreed upon; but by now Oo-gloo, having cooled down a bit, insisted that if the Musks won the *Frisco Maid* would be allowed to depart only after unloading all but a very scant supply of rations. So Stewie was not the only one who would suffer should our team meet defeat.

Stewie himself came into our meeting a trifle late. When he heard of the scheduled game he was hilariously enthused, and as equally depressed upon learning the specified terms. "That's fine an' dandy—if we win!" he exclaimed dolefully. "But if we lose, then what about me?"

"In that case," replied Captain Boyer not unkindly, "if I were in your place I'd devote a large portion of my time in praying for an east wind."

Well, that very next morning the wind changed—but *not* to the east. It came straight from the north, and its icy blast seemed to chill us to the marrow. Up to this time it had only been forty or fifty degrees below zero; now goodness only knows how cold it did get.

Those Peroxides didn't seem to notice the cold at all, and early that morning the Musks got orders to report at the ball park for a try-out. I went along with them. With me was a garrulous young person named Blarz—a sort of village cut-up—who had taken a fancy to me seemingly, and took it upon himself a fancy to me seemingly, and took it upon himself that I be given a true line on all sporting events and conditions locally, both past, present, and future. At that, this Blarz was rather an interesting lad, and I was glad enough to hear his sport dope, believing such portions of it as I thought best to believe.

The park was located about half a league from the village, in a sort of hollow or natural amphitheater, with a ledge of huge ice cliffs surrounding on three sides. On the remaining side of the field a high snow wall had been built, thus inclosing completely the rectangular space. There was a regulation diamond, with pads for bases made of skins stuffed with moss. In the ice cliff back of home plate, tier above tier, seats had been carved out for a grand stand, and at either side were the bleachers. There was a clubhouse out beyond center field, and from this building we presently saw the Musks come bounding forth.

I looked upon them with strangely conflicting emotions. It thrilled me—as a devotee of the best in athletics—to gaze upon such splendid specimens, yet now there was a new-formed doubt and anxiety in my mind as well. They were as fine a bunch of ball players as I ever looked upon—tall, trim, quick, agile as slim panthers; they went about their work as though to the manner born, champions from the ground up.

"Well, there they are!" exclaimed young Blarz with conscious pride. "What d'yuh think of 'em?"

"It's a little early yet to express an opinion," I answered, determined not to let him know just to what extent I was already affected. "They look like players, but they've got to show me!"

They had discarded heavy furs for neat uniforms of deerskin, and so quick were they in their movements, so violent their exertions, the cold had absolutely no effect upon them. Down in my heart came a sad misgiving as I watched them, and the thought came to my mind more than once: "Poor Stewie!"

They batted up fungo flies, ran bases, practiced sliding, and worked out details of inside play. The surgeon turned to me with an awed expression. "Moggs, *where* did these rummies get that stuff?" And I answered him: "You've got me, Oscar. What they're pulling out there right now ain't six months behind the New York Giants, and I'll take an oath to it!"

We watched in silence for a few minutes the wonderful stunts being put over out there on that hard-frozen diamond; then the surgeon turned to me again with the observation: "The cap'n was talking with one of the tribe's old-timers yesterday. This village patriarch—a hundred years old he was, at least—told him how years and years ago, when he himself was a mere lad, a great bag with a basket attached came down out of the sky, and from this basket there alighted a number of big, blond-bearded men who spoke a strange tongue and who brought with them strange instruments. Now, Moggs, doesn't it seem not altogether impossible that the coming of these scientific adventurers—hopelessly stranded, and perhaps, after years, mating with the native women— was the beginning of this strange race we find here to-day, who speak our language and bear the physical semblance of those early adventurers? Of course, from time to time, too, they must have come in contact with civilization in some manner——"

His line of reasoning and deduction was cut short

by the approach of Wa-glum-too, the stalwart captain of the Musks, who came to courteously offer us the use of the field should the Seals be ready for a work-out. We thanked him, but declined the offer. "Then," he said, turning to go, "I'll just let some of my pitchers warm up a bit."

A tall, sinewy young giant stepped into the pitcher's box and began carelessly lobbing them over to a little squat catcher back of home plate. Soon he began putting a little something on the ball, and he began to burn 'em through.

"Who's that pitcher?" I asked of Blarz.

"Some class to that kid, hey?" he said, ignoring my query.

"What's his name?"

"Bearson; he led the league last year by a big margin."

I could not take my eyes off him for an instant. Seeing how absorbed I had become in the young slab artist, Blarz fairly outdid himself in expatiating. "He's got some delivery, believe me! Speed! Say, nothin' to it! And a fast ball with a hop to it, and a fade-away that is a dream!"

"What's his best ball?" I asked.

Blarz was silent for a moment. I surmised—and rightly—that he was getting primed to "string" me. Say, that boy could have pulled down a big salary as a sporting scribe on a big sheet! Finally he answered complacently: "His 'best' ball? Well, he got so many it's hard to say offhand, but I like best myself his 'spike' ball."

"'Spike' ball, hey?"

"You bettcha! Ever hear of it?"

"Never; what's it like?"

"The 'spike,'" he resumed gravely, "is sure one heartbreaker for the fence busters——"

"They can't connect with it?"

"Naw; they can't even see it!"

"Well, well! How's it thrown!"

Blarz was in his element now. "The 'spike,'" he went on, "can only be used in such a country as this."

"Why?"

"It depends on the weather, see?"

"No; not clearly."

"Well, the 'spike' ball is prepared in this way: First Bearson takes a dipper of freshly melted snow; then he closes the fingers of his right hand—not too closely—and places his fist against the ball, thumb upward; this leaves a funnellike opening, inclosed by his fingers, and down this funnel he pours the melted snow. Now, remember, with the temperature somewhere around fifty or sixty below, this snow freezes instantly, leaving a firm *spike* sticking out from the ball. Bearson makes two of these; these he grips when ready to throw, and the leverage thus attained is tremendous. With this advantage, Bearson can throw a twister that would make one of Alexander's seem without a kink!"

I looked up at him searchingly. Not a muscle of face so much as quivered; his expression was one of innocence, and wholly inscrutable.

"Some ball!" I commented at length.

"Isn't it, though? But Bearson seldom uses the 'spike'—only when he's in a bad hole——"

"Why not?"

"Too dangerous."

"For whom?"

"The catcher."

"How's that?"

"Well, you see, when the batter fails to connect—as he does ten times out of twelve—it makes an unhappy time for the backstop trying to handle that 'spike' ball——"

At that instant I saw Bearson getting ready to quit the box. "Blarz," I said, breaking into another imaginative flight most likely, "I want to meet that young pitcher. Can you fix it?"

"Sure I will," he responded. "Come along with me."

I met Bearson, of the Borealis League, a few minutes later in the clubhouse, and I imparted to him certain information that made his blue eyes glisten with boyish delight and eagerness. But my enthusiasm over the proposition we had in view was fully equal to his own. We left the park together a few minutes after that to hold an important confab with Chief Oo-gloo.

That night I dropped around to see Captain Boyer. I found him in a state of mental depression and anxiety.

"Moggs," he began at once, "if I ever get out of this mess I'll take a sacred vow never to bring on board another sealskin——"

"What's wrong?" I asked.

"Wrong! Why, most everything. My men are in desperate straits, though some don't seem to realize it. My cook is likely to meet a terrible fate. Then, too, I feel that I haven't been exactly fair with you——"

"In what regard?"

"Well—about this ivory business——"

"Don't let that worry you for a minute."

"But you have found no ivory——"

"You're wrong; I have!"

He looked at me in amazement, and I resumed: "Listen—I told you I was an 'ivory hunter'; I am. I'm a baseball scout for the Pacific Coast League."

"No!"

"Fact. I've been trying for some time to locate a good pitcher for Boss McCredie—of the Portland Beavers. From time to time rumors have been floating down from the Far North about some good talent up there in those frozen wastes——"

"And you set out with me, looking for ball players?"

"I did."

"A crazy, wild-goose hunt," he commented.

"No; not a bit of it. I've found the man I want; he's going back with me—if things turn out a certain way. I have Oo-gloo's consent, though I'll admit he feels safe enough—under the stipulations—in promising I may take the man back with me."

"And this player——"

"Is Pitcher Bearson," I answered, "of the Borealis League."

IV.

SATURDAY came. During the forenoon the sun shone out, but only for an hour or so; then it ducked back out of sight, leaving us gray twilight. The game, scheduled to start at noon, had brought forth a crowd that packed and jammed the grand stand, bleachers, and overflowed into the field. Just before the start of the contest, the aurora borealis burst forth across the drab sky, lighting up the ball park with radiant, dazzling brilliancy. The ice pinnacles of the inclosure glittered alternately blue and crimson; the effect was weird, bizarre, uncanny.

In so low a temperature our Seals would have been simply out of the running right from the start, had it not been for an ingenious device rigged up by the ship's electrician. He fitted out for each player—and substitute—a contrivance of fine wire, which was worn close to the body beneath the outer clothing. To each network of wire he attached a small, portable storage battery. When the wearer began suffering with the intense cold and felt himself becoming numb, he simply turned a switch, and a warm glow at once started permeating his whole being! Of course care had to be exercised so that the switch could be turned off before the clothing caught fire. That little invention of the ship's electrician—unknown, of course, to the Peroxides—sent the Seals into the fray in fine fighting form. Not only were they immune from the bitter cold, but the intermittent shots of electricity seemed to supply a noticeable ginger and "pep" that was truly a delight to us of the *Frisco Maid* to behold.

In some strange, unaccountable manner, news of the great game had reached far into the interior, and a number of alien tribes were in attendance—squat, flat-nosed people—who, strangely enough, rooted lustily all the way, individually and collectively, for the Seals to win. They didn't gain admittance to the park without paying, either; in fact, each contributed either a skin or piece of ivory or some article of value before being allowed through the sacred portals. By the time the game was about to start there was a pile of ivory tusks outside the gate nearly as high as the wall. We learned that this ivory had been dug out of great blocks of solid ice, together with the almost perfectly preserved forms of early-day mammoths. The captain of the *Frisco Maid* was so taken up with this huge pile of ivory tusks we could scarcely get him inside to see the game.

Just at high noon the umpire, chosen from a neighboring clan, and supposedly neutral, strode out to the plate, adjusted his walrus-hide chest protector, removed his cap, and turned to the eager, expectant throng: "Ladies an' g'men—batt'ries for to-day's game—Musks, Unglub an' Bearson; for the Seals, Clancy an' Moore!" A mighty cheer arose. The umpire took a small fox tail from his hind pocket, whisked the snow from home plate, and called forth: "Play ball!" The great game was on.

The Musks, perhaps to make the most of the fleeting light, chose first turn at bat. The Seals took the field.

The first batter up was Ugh-oo-las-koo, the Musk center fielder. Ugh had finished the season with the very commendable batting average of .366, and he hadn't forgotten about it. He came striding up to the plate trailing a huge bat carved out of driftwood. He was some tough mug. His cap was pulled down over his left eye; he glared at our pitcher, Clancy; he expectorated fiercely and bawled out through the corner of his mouth: "Shoot 'er over, Busher; I've been eatin' up yer kind all season!"

Clancy looked at him sort of surprised; then that Irish boy lit into him: "Why, you poor Swede squab," he began, "if I wasn't afraid of denting the ball, I'd 'bean' you one, jes' for luck! Say, how'd you get out here, anyhow? Shut your eyes and swing at this one; it's your only chance!"

The ball came on a line with the batter' head. Ugh ducked back quickly. The ball, breaking sharply, curved in and downward over the plate. "S-strike one!" yelled the umpire.

Ugh-oo-las-koo had never been up against pitching like that before. He seemed sort of dazed by it, but he got a firmer grip on his big bat, and stood poised for the next one. Clancy cut loose another, similar in all respects to his first offering. This time, with the instinct of a born hitter, Ugh stepped forward and met the ball before the break. He soaked it square on the nose; it sailed on out toward the pinnacles which still gleamed blue and crimson, and it sailed on past—for a homer!

You should have heard that fur-trimmed home crowd yell; a tumult of riotous rejoicing worthy of the occasion. Ugh trotted complacently around the bases. As he rounded third he looked over and grinned at Clancy, and the latter, taking it all good-naturedly, called out to him: "You're there, son; you outguessed me that time a mile!"

Well, it was a bad inning for our pitcher; he couldn't get to going right. For one thing, he was having trouble with his storage battery—so we learned later—the wires either getting hot enough to roast him alive or else refusing to work at all. When the side was finally retired, the Musks had chalked up three runs, and a mighty roar went up from their rooters; then, when this died away, a shrill, feminine voice piped up from the grand stand: "Never mind that, Clancy, boy; you'll hold 'em next inning!" And Clancy, walking over to the bench, turned very red; but maybe he didn't pitch his heart out the rest of that game!

The Seals came to bat. Foster, first up, was out on a sizzling drive to left that looked, at the start, good for three bases; a long run and circus catch by Grumph put a crimp in that drive. The next man up singled; the batter following walked. It was easy to see that Bearson was having trouble with his salary wing, and he was overanxious.

Now, as was known only to Chief Oo-gloo and myself, the position the Musk pitcher was in was almost tragic. I have never known anything similar to it. You see, he was determined to *win*, and yet, had he but known it, a victory for the Musks meant that he would *not* be permitted to go back with me to Portland. Chief Oo-gloo had consented to let him go only upon the condition that the Seals win from him! And there he was now—poor, brave-hearted young pitcher—trying his best to accomplish that which, if achieved, would mean but the frustrating of his highest hope and ambition!

The side was finally retired, but we had tied up the score, making it three to three. We blanked the Musks in their half. Clancy was going better now—due either to better insulation or the encouragement of the little blond girlie in the grand stand—and he mowed down the heavy-hitting Musks in one-two-three order.

The game rocked along until the eighth, with neither

side able to get another run across the pan; then the flues of Clancy's heating contrivance seemed to clog again. He grew cold and numb, and could scarcely grasp the ball. He finished the inning on sheer nerve, but the Musks nicked him for a single, a pass, and a double, which pushed another run over. He held them tight in their first of the ninth, and we came to bat with the score four to three against us.

The way young Bearson was breezing along now that one run lead seemed as good as a million, but the Seals came in determined to sew the game up again at least. Stewie, playing at second, was awfully depressed now, and began begging his fellow players to start a rally. Oscar, the surgeon, was out on the coaching line, waving his arms frantically and shouting out: "Come on now, Seals! Get into 'em, lads; you can do it! You, Thompson—give us a hit, son, an' start 'er rolling!"

But Thompson fouled out to third. Wagstaff, next up, drove a stinging single through short. A chorus of cheers—mostly high soprano—came from the grand stand; but the next batter hit to third, and Wagstaff was got at second by an eyelash. It was a close play; the Seals swarmed around the umpire noisily, but he waved them back.

The blazing lights on the distant ice pinnacles had turned now to an evil, ominous green; the tints of the borealis were dying rapidly. It all seemed prophetic of our speedy finish. With two down, the turned now to an evil, ominous green; the tints of endeavoring to worry Bearson.

Stewie came to bat. Many a time has a pitcher, striding up to the plate, been called upon to win his own game; but here was a batter whose very life depended now upon his own individual effort. It was a strained and tense moment. A hush fell over the throng; it was broken by a pitiful, despairing voice— the heart-torn plea of a blond widow to whom our cookie had paid some marked attention during our enforced sojourn among the Peroxides: "Oh, Mr. Stewie—please, *please* line 'er out!"

Bearson was going strong now and pitching superbly. The ball flashed across the plate.

"S-strike one!" yelled the umpire.

Cheers and groans alternately from the crowd, and the big voice of old Chief Oo-gloo calling out: "Jes' a little farther to go, son; hold 'em—hold 'em tight!"

On the second pitched ball, the runner on first darted to second, and, after a long slide, came up just ahead of the ball. He was safe; but Stewie, to confuse the catcher had swung at the ball. Now there were two strikes against him!

The blond girls in the grand stand, no longer giggling, began a low, mournful sort of chant. Say, it sounded creepy! We saw that it was bothering Bearson, too. He was getting restless and fidgety, and didn't seem able to get Unglaub's signals. He threw the ball; it went wide. The catcher snapped it back to him savagely. The chant continued, louder, more penetrating. Bearson was beginning to break under the spell of it, and the ball he threw struck in front of the plate. Unglaub snatched it up, and carried it out upon the mound, and what he said to the young pitcher made little wreaths of white smoke curl up all around the box. But again he failed to

get the ball over, and it stood two strikes and three balls.

Now it was up to Stewie. He bent lower over the plate; he grasped his big bat a little tighter. The yellow sheen on the pinnacles of ice flickered and went out, and from the grand stand, weird, mournful, came the Chant of Departed Souls.

Bearson threw the ball. "*C-r-a-c-k!*" went Stewie's bat. The ball sailed high in the air, straight for center field. The Seal rooters jumped up with a glad shout; it ended in a despairing wail of anguish. The ball was coming down straight into the hands of Ugh-oo-las-koo, who stood calmly, confidently awaiting it.

At that instant I saw Oscar, the ship's surgeon, rush out along the side lines. He picked up a great, sharp-pointed icicle; on the point of this he placed a huge snowball; he touched a match to the mass of snow; it *began blazing fiercely!*

Waving the snowball torch high in the air, the surgeon called out wildly to Ugh-oo-las-koo. The center fielder heard him. He looked over to the side lines. His hands dropped to his sides; his mouth flew open in amazement. The ball came down, 'beaned' him square on the dome, and rolled off over the snow toward deep center. Stewie and the runner ahead of him both scored, and the valiant Seals from the little *Frisco Maid* had triumphed over the strong and husky Musk Oxen with a score of five to four!

V.

THE Peroxides and the alien tribes were so taken up with the burning-snowball stunt of Oscar's that all thought of the game's sudden and unexpected termination was, for the nonce, cast aside. They wanted the surgeon to repeat; he refused flatly. He told them that the burning snow was "big medicine," only to be pulled once in a lifetime.

As for the ball game, we knew well enough we had won on a mere fluke, but the Musks and that team's supporters were good sports and good losers. They had no alibi to offer; our ball players were the heroes of the hour. They were made much of, especially by certain erstwhile chanters. Little groups were scattered here and there, talking over the game and Oscar's spectacular stunt, when suddenly, from the far end of the field, a ringing cheer went up. The sound became a universal shout—an anthem of praise. The wind had changed; it was blowing straight from the east!

A week later the *Frisco Maid* was safely afloat again. We had come with fifteen men, and we departed with exactly the same number, including the exuberant and rejoicing Bearson, of the Borealis League; but we left without Stewie. After all we'd gone through to save him, he elected of his own will and accord to remain behind. Needless to say, the little blond widow who had rooted so hard for him during the big game had more than a little to do with the final decision of the rosy-cheeked cook. After many and ardent farewells, we sailed away from the strange, mysterious land of the Peroxides, homeward bound again.

On the way back down through the North Sea we ran straight into that U. S. revenue cutter. They made us haul to, and boarded us. Before leaving, however, Captain Boyer, with customary sagacity and foresight, had traded all the sealskins for the ivory tusks collected by Chief Oo-gloo as admission fees to the ball game. The officers from the cutter went all through our little ship; then they apologized for having detained us. Our captain accepted this apology with grave and quiet dignity.

A month later we safely entered Frisco Bay. Before leaving the ship, Captain Boyer called me into his cabin for a little refreshment. "Moggs," he said genially as we clinked glasses, "we've had a successful voyage; we both brought back good 'ivory.' I am well satisfied, as I know you are, too. There is just one thing that I can't quite understand, and which I have thought over no little——"

"What is that, cap'n?" I broke in.

"That little incident of the burning snow!" he replied gravely.

"Simple enough—when you understand," I replied. "You see, Oscar is a firm believer in preparedness. He didn't know just what sort of a mix we might be in before that game ended, so he came prepared for any eventuality. Now, that snow—before he touched a match to it—was plenteously sprinkled with *camphor pellets!* If you have any doubts about snow burning under such conditions, just try it some time. I can honestly say that it was the quick wit and ingenuity of our surgeon which saved the day for us and brought the triumph of defeat to Pitcher Bearson——"

"To Oscar, the surgeon!" broke in the captain, raising his glass, "and his torch of burning snow!"

LILITH

By Roy Le Moyne

AH, Lilith, let us twine these flowers
   Around the day's sweet sanctity
While Love strings all the shining hours
   Upon the flesh's rosary . . . . . .
For things turn back that now are ours
   Into a growing yesterday.

Come, let us speak of lovely things
   Close to our hearts while yet we may,
For Night shall wrap her star-strewn wings
   About us when we go our way . . . . . .
All songs turn back that Love now sings
   Into a growing yesterday.

A time comes when the heart is fed
   Upon the things we build to-day
And things unfinished and unsaid
   Shall rise to scorn, and well they may . . . . .
Then Love shall stand among the dead
   Who haunt the growing yesterday.

The Jeweled Ibis
By J.C. Kofoed

CHAPTER I.
SOMETHING OF MYSTERY.

WHEN Dave Hudson walked into the United States consulate at Alexandria the night the leaky old *Mozambique* foundered the consul was so startled that he nearly swallowed his cigar. In reality, only Dave's failure to appear should have surprised him. Every sailorman from Bangkok to Liverpool knew Hudson for the strongest, bravest, and luckiest dare-devil that sailed the Seven Seas. The consul knew it, too, but he had counted a three-mile swim through a heavy storm beyond even Dave's extraordinary powers of endurance.

Though bruised and soaking wet from his buffet with the sea, Hudson wore his eternally cheerful grin. He was a big, nut-brown chap, with hair crisped tawny by the sun, and a jaw whose breadth proclaimed the only yellow streak he possessed to be in his hair.

His visit lasted only until morning. A major in the Sudanese corps—a man named Helim—had deserted with enough papers to plunge Britain into a native war, and an expedition was hastily preparing to follow him. As he could not secure a berth on any of the ships in port, Hudson joined them. The colonel warned him at the time that the chase would take them across the Libyan Desert, perhaps even to the gates of forbidden Jarabub, where no Christian had ever been.

Six months later Hudson limped into Alexandria alone and in rags. The deserter apparently had many friends among the *shenzis*—wild men—for ambuscades had been frequent. Broken by numberless savage attacks, the pursuers had been easy victims of the desert.

The novelty of the ancient empire no longer gripped Dave. On the contrary, the bazaars, the clack of many tongues, and the stench of camels grew intolerable. He had brought nothing back with him except a knowledge of the Egyptian tongue and mannerisms, so his need of a job became imperative. As luck would have it, the opportunity of signing on a freighter bound for London presented itself, and Hudson snapped it up. Later he regretted his haste.

The work itself was not particularly hard. English skippers are slacker taskmasters than their Yankee cousins, but they lack the American largeness of soul. They are petty in their discipline; they pay wretchedly; and the food they supply is vilely worm-eaten and bitter. Hudson made no complaint. His stomach had been insulted too often to rebel at anything remotely eatable.

He found it more difficult to get along with Captain Cullen, however. In his years of seafaring Dave had sailed with thieves and brutes in the cabin, but Cullen was the worst of the lot. The jackal and the pig struggled in his face. He bulldozed and heckled the men from morning till night.

Late in the afternoon of their third day out from Alexandria, Hudson lay stretched out in the bottom of the captain's gig, smoking his pipe and enjoying the cool breeze. He was wondering how he could make money—big money. Silver had always been quicksilver in Dave's fingers, so this sudden desire to accumulate a share of the world's goods certainly suggested an ulterior motive.

He had spent his last night ashore with the amiable consul. He remembered that night vividly. It was not until nearly twelve o'clock that he had started for his own quarters. The narrow streets were quite dark. From the darkest and narrowest of these he had heard the sound of panting breaths and scuffling feet, and then, for an instant, the fear-smothered voice of a woman.

The struggle was in a little hovel at the end of the alley, and Hudson projected his six foot of bone and sinew into the fray with the speed of a Mauser bullet. A half dozen *fellaheen* had attacked an American girl and her servant, but, being as cowardly as they were ruffianly, they stampeded for the door at the first sign of his prowess.

The girl—whose name was Marian Chandler—appeared tremendously grateful. Though dusty and disheveled, her beauty transcended such obstacles and impressed itself on Dave as the most wonderful he had ever seen. She was about twenty, he judged, but there was nothing of the callow débutante about her. She looked one straight in the eyes, and shook hands with a sincere grip.

She had supplied the motive for Hudson's desire to accumulate wealth. He had met pretty girls before, but none who gave him that peculiar, confused sort of a thrill that Miss Chandler did. As she was rich, he did not think it would be honorable to try for her favor unless he was equally independent.

Lying there on his back, he grinned up at the sky, but it was a wistful sort of a grin.

Two men came along the deck. Without troubling to look up, Hudson knew who they were. One, by the clatter of hobnailed shoes, was Cullen, and the walloping of bare feet on the boards proclaimed his companion to be Toni, the coal-black Sudanese cook.

"Now, look 'ere, Toni," the captain was saying in his slovenly cockney dialect, "if y' keep up yer cursed chatter y'll never see yer wench again, I'll l'y ten to two on that. Y're in on the deal if y' keep a still tongue in yer head and let the rum alone. If y' don't——" His pause was full of menace.

"Thass all right, boss," said Toni, with a drunken snicker. He had an accent like a North Carolina darky and a voice that carried around the ship. "I know sumthin' 'bout this Ra an' the jeweled-ibis bizness——"

"Silence, y' fool! Would y' have every bleedin' tyke in the fo'cas'le guessin' the secret then? Y' know too much as 'tis."

"I know this much," said the cook, and he began to chant throatily:

"Sesostris, mighty ruler,
Has hid de secret in
Hebben-sent boss of Upper an' Lower Egypt,
De belly ob de ibis——"

The illiterate dirge ended in a shriek of pain and a gurgle. Hudson sprang to his feet, an instant too late to save the Sudanese. Cullen seized Toni by the throat, and with a heave of his hairy ape arms flung him over the side. Dave caught a glimpse of his black, agonized face in the swirl of foam before he disappeared.

"That was murder!" declared the engineer grimly.

He stood upright, bracing his tall, muscular body against the roll of the ship, and glared down at Cullen like an accusing Nemesis. There was something unclean about the captain that rasped on Hudson like a rough singlet. He was repulsive as a vulture.

Dave repeated aggressively: "That was murder!"

Cullen turned a pair of coldly expressionless eyes

on him. "Blimey if it was," he denied. "It goes down in the log as mutiny, and ye'll 'ave to admit, Mr. 'Udson, that Toni was a mutinous dog. Nobody'll miss the likes o' 'im, and ye'll forget 'im, too, d'ye hear; ye'll forget 'im, too."

With a shrug indicative of contempt, the engineer jumped out of the gig and walked away. Though he did not turn around, he could feel the captain staring malevolently at his back.

Afterward Hudson wondered as to the origin of the quarrel between Cullen and his cook. It was evident—from Toni's chant—that they shared a secret concerning Sesostris, a several-thousand-year-dead king, and the ibis—the sacred bird of Egypt.

How they were connected with this illiterate cockney and his half-savage Sudanese henchman was more than he could figure out. It was too grotesque for serious thought. Before they sighted England he had almost forgotten it.

There was no more trouble until the *Asian* puffed into her dock. It is the custom for sailors, who are "picked up on the beach," as the saying goes, to be paid off at the end of the trip and not to be taken back to the starting place unless they re-sign. Hudson had no desire to take another voyage, so he went down to the captain's cabin for his pay on the evening of their docking.

Cullen was sitting at his desk, tracing a plan on a dirty map. He looked up with a leer. "What d'ye want?"

"My wages."

"Yer wiges, eh? Well, me bird, ye'll be ashippin' along o' me back to Port Said, won't y'? Y' won't need no wiges till y' get there."

Though slow to anger, Dave's temper rose at this culmination of a particularly nasty voyage. But he knew that if he was going to get any money he would have to be careful.

"I beg your pardon, sir," he said as cheerfully as he could. "I'm going to lie over in London a bit, and then sign on an American ship. My home is in New York, and I haven't seen the old place for pretty close to ten years——"

With that Cullen's face turned a dirty sort of purple, and he jumped up. "I don't give a shillin' 'ow long ye've been aw'y from 'ome, 'Udson," he yelled, slapping his hand down on the map. "I need men, and 'arf the bloody crew 'as slung their 'ook already. D'ye think I want to ship a lot o' dirty dockers for this trip? The gime's too bloody big for that trash. Now listen a bit." His voice descended to a wheedling whisper. "Ye've been to Sa-el-Hagar—once ancient Sais—aven't y'?"

"Yes."

"W'y?"

That sort of questioning did not appear to be leading up to payment, and Hudson needed the money badly. So he said in a brusque tone: "I've gone over a good part of Egypt in the past few years, and Sa-el-Hagar is only one o' a 'undred towns I've visited."

"Y' know more than ye'll s'y, I'll l'y two to one on that," said the captain, nodding craftily. "Now gi'e me a str'ight answer. Ye've met Se-hotep-ab-Ra, aven't ye—or that feller Chandler?"

Chandler! The name struck a responsive chord in

Hudson's heart, and it is possible a reflection of it showed in his face. But he did not know any men by that name, so he answered in the negative. As for Se-hotep-ab-Ra, Dave had never heard of him.

"Well, then," continued Cullen, "what do y' know about the priests of the Theban Zeus, o' Sesostris an' his secret, o' the jeweled ibis——

"Nothing!" cried the engineer. "And I don't want to. Give me the money due me and let me go."

There was an ugly-looking knife lying on the desk, and Cullen picked it up. "Y' know too bloody much, an' y' c'n take yer choice o' comin' wi' me or kippin' on the bottom o' the Thames. Fer all I know that feller Chandler might 'ave y' in his p'y." Apparently the thought frightened him. He jumped forward, with his teeth showing like a jackal's and the weapon swinging in his hand.

He found it harder to handle the American than the Sudanese, however. Hudson side-stepped and jolted him in the solar plexus with one fist, while he uppercut him with the other. Cullen went down in a heap on the floor. He clawed and scrambled around in an effort to get his breath back and yell for help. Knowing there was no longer any hope of getting what was due him, Dave put on his greasy cap and walked out of the door. The first officer, a man named Grawley, tried to stop him, but Hudson gave him a taste of the same medicine he had doled out to Cullen. In five minutes he left the ship and docks behind him.

It is not pleasant, of course, to lose all one's possession and be set adrift in London with only a tu'-pence in one's pockets, but the rugged American was too optimistic to worry about that. The only thing he regretted was that, in all probability, he would never know how the secret of Sesostris—whatever it was—happened to be mixed up with a jeweled ibis and the priests of the Theban Zeus and Cullen and Chandler and Ra and all the rest of them. But if he had stayed on the *Asian* and tried to find out they would have had a knife between his shoulder blades sooner or later. He was certain of that.

CHAPTER II.

IN THE DARKNESS.

IT was one of those nasty, wet nights that are so frequent during the English autumn. Hudson walked through labyrinths of filthy streets, where it was dangerous for a well-dressed man to go, but no one paid any particular attention to him. The slop chest of the *Asian* did not furnish purple and fine linen. His clothes were as worn as that of any denizen of the district, and he was soaked to the skin. Sailors down on their luck are common enough in the East End.

The American consulate was his intended haven. A mate who had lost an arm in the Chinese troubles was some sort of a clerk there, and Dave was sure of a hearty welcome from him. As it happened, however, he did not get within miles of the consulate or genial Marty Mallory.

By the time the engineer reached Spitalfields Garden the rain had slackened, and he sat down on one of the benches. He had been doing the hardest kind of work since three in the morning, and even his almost tireless muscles had begun to feel the strain.

Except for the flicker of an arc light, it was pretty dark there, and it was too chilly and wet to get any rest. So, after a few moments, he rose, squeezed the water from his cap, and started off.

He had not taken ten steps before a girl came running toward him down the narrow, graveled path—a pretty slip of a maid, with dark, frightened eyes and the sweetest lips man ever longed for. She gasped with relief when she saw Dave's keen, bronzed face. In a moment she was in front of him, with her hand trembling on his arm.

Years of world wandering had taught Hudson to mask his emotions. Though he was astounded beyond words, he merely smiled and took off his cap. "Good evening, Miss Chandler," he said. His heart commenced playing him the same tricks as it had when he first met her in Alexandria.

"For God's sake, help me!" she panted. "They're at my heels, and this is my last chance. Take this"—she pressed something into his hands—"and carry it to Mr. Drexel Chandler at the Ritz Carlton. Will you do this for me?"

"I would do anything for you," said the seaman, not noticing how obvious were his words.

"Oh, thank you! Guard it with your life, Mr. Hudson. It is the jeweled ibis!" Then, in a flash, she was gone.

The jeweled ibis again! Now what the deuce did it mean? The ibis, of course, was a cranelike bird sacred to the Egyptians, but what that had to do with the bundle in his hand or the quarrel that had led to the murder of Toni he could not, for the life of him, understand.

He walked under the arc light to examine the thing that had been intrusted to him. The wrappings had fallen off, and in his palm lay an image of the ibis. It was probably six inches high, made of hard black wood—ebony, most likely—and was inlaid from the tip of the curved beak to the claws with most exquisite jewels. It must have been worth thousands upon thousands of dollars, entirely aside from its value as an antique. But the value of the thing only added a more opaque tint to the mystery.

What was Marian Chandler doing in the East End, and how could she be mixed up in the same affair as Captain Cullen? What was this mystery that generated murders and pursuits and the trusting of a penniless sailorman with priceless jewels? But—and a smile lit his bronzed face—the girl *had* trusted him. That was a guerdon of honor, and he intended seeing the ibis safely in the hands of the man for whom it was intended.

There came a pattering of feet along the path, and the engineer hastily wrapped the gem in its covering and thrust it into his pocket. The police would take it from him as quickly as the little lady's pursuers. They would not believe that a poor man could come by such a thing honestly.

But it was not a "bobby" who ran down the path of Spitalfields Garden. It was a burly man, whose coat only partly hid his evening clothes. He was an extraordinarily ugly chap, with a flat, wide nose, thick lips, and fierce yellow eyes. He hesitated for an instant when he saw Hudson, then walked over with an odd sort of a smile.

"Might I inquire, sir," he asked in English with

an Oxford accent, "if you saw a lady pass by? I will make it worth your while if you will point out the way she took." He peered searchingly at Dave, who had drawn back in the shadows. There was something puzzling in his attitude.

"I couldn't tell you," said Hudson quietly. .

The man—who looked like a *shenzi* from Nubia, for all his fine clothes—took a step nearer. A sudden stealthy softness came into his voice. "You *do* know," he sibilated, "and, by Zeus, the greatest of all gods, I will force you to tell! Did you think I had not penetrated your disguise, Hudson effendi? Your time in Egypt was not spent for pleasure. It is Chandler who employs you, and for him you seek to penetrate the secret of Sesostris. Is it not so?"

"I don't know what you're talking about," said Hudson, exasperated, "and I don't give a tinker's continental, my friend. Take your hand off my arm. Another knife, eh?"

The brown man struck him in the face with all his strength, and Hudson went to his knees, dazed. Before he could struggle up the *shenzi* was at his throat. Now, Hudson was as strong a man as ever sailed the seas, and but for that first treacherous blow he might have overmastered his enemy. As it was, he was bent backward by the dark man, who tried to get his knife hand free. Hudson did not lose his head and struggle frantically, but concentrated his efforts on keeping the weapon away. But his assailant was as strong as the sacred bull, and, inch by inch, the blade crept nearer.

In those moments the only thing Hudson regretted was that Marian had found him a broken reed and that she would lose her jewel after all. He had been in too many tight places during his adventurous career to admit defeat before he had to, but he nearly admitted it then. He hardly expected a policeman to appear. They were too busy making ragged wanderers move on to stop a murder in the heart of London town. His life depended on his own slowly waning strength.

The knife continued its slow and jerky, but terribly inevitable journey toward Hudson's throat. The African's dark, twisted face was close to his. He meant to kill Dave, and nothing but a miracle could stop him.

The miracle happened!

A shadow slipped along the sharp-spiked iron railing surrounding the garden. Dave felt a body brush by him. Then his assailant's head jerked back, a great puffing sigh escaped his lips, and the knife dropped from his nerveless hand. For a moment he stood swaying like a drunken man, a blot of blood creeping out of his hair into his eyes. Then his knees buckled under him, and he sank in a dreadfully contorted heap on the sidewalk.

Panting for breath, Hudson straightened up in time to see his rescuer vault the body and speed away in the darkness. In that fleeting instant he caught a glimpse of the lean, ascetic profile of a man of say five and thirty—an utter stranger. And yet—yet— there was something vaguely familiar about that face —something——

Pausing only to ascertain that the supposed Nubian was still breathing, Hudson hastened away. It was a prison matter if he was found with the unconscious man at his feet. Besides, he was anxious to complete

his trust and deliver the jeweled ibis to Mr. Drexel Chandler.

It was a long walk through the rain, but Dave was so engrossed with his thoughts that he totally ignored the physical discomfort. He was wondering about this fellow, Chandler. Ordinarily his concern would have been with the man who attacked him, but this puzzle superseded that one in interest. Was Chandler, by any quirk of an unkind fate, Marian's husband? The thought stirred his heart into turmoil. He wanted that girl as he had never wanted anything in his life. And if she were free he would work his fingers to the bone for the money that would enable him to support a wife. But if she were married—— The thought depressed him, and he tried to forget it.

When he halted at last in the garish glow of the big hotel he felt rather diffident about entering. His slop-chest clothes were wrinkled and soaking wet, and he looked as though he had been "padding the hoof" for a thousand miles.

He overcame that momentary hesitation, and, squaring his broad shoulders, walked up the steps. A few overdressed people laughed, and a shocked clerk tried to hurry him out, but Dave Hudson wasn't the hurrying kind. His keen, weather-bronzed face, topped with its tawny mane, made an impression that was furthered by his incisive manner of speaking. After murmuring, "preposterous" and "unprecedented," the clerk agreed to send a note up to Mr. Chandler, being assured that it really was a matter of life and death.

The note Dave scrawled was calculated to gain admittance, though decidedly brief. He wrote: "I must see you at once on important business," and signed it, "The man with the jeweled ibis." A boy carried it up to Mr. Chandler's suite.

The "buttons"—grown suddenly obsequious—came down presently and escorted Hudson to the lift. When they reached the fourth floor another personage in blue and gold took him in hand and led him through a maze of corridors to what was, he learned later, the most expensive suite of rooms in the hotel.

A studious-looking man of say five and thirty, with an alert, nervous manner, threw open the door. It was the identical chap who had saved Hudson from the *shenzi* in Spitalfields Garden.

"Mr. Drexel Chandler, sir," announced the servant, and to the gentleman in the door, "Mr. 'Udson, sir."

Dave drew a deep breath, but repressed any exhibition of surprise. Apparently there were even more angles to the affair than he had believed.

"Good evening," he said quietly. "I didn't expect to see you again quite so soon."

CHAPTER III.

NOT KNOWN.

COME in," said Chandler in a voice he tried to make unconcerned, but which trembled nevertheless. He was arrayed in dressing gown and slippers, and betrayed no signs of having been out in the unhospitable elements. "Your note"—he crushed it in his slim white fingers—"was rather ambiguous. What is it you want?"

The engineer did not answer at once. He was gauging Drexel Chandler, and when he studied a man he did it thoroughly and slowly. Chandler's face possessed an aristocratic thinness of line that spoke plainly of good blood. His lips were cleanly shaped, if a trifle hard, and his eyes were frank and wide apart. His features were the masculine counterparts of Marian's, and Hudson felt suddenly relieved. The man was her brother; every sign pointed to it.

It was apparent to the most casual that he was near the limit of nervous repression. His hands twitched, and he paced the room like a caged leopard. Dave felt a thrill of sorrow for him. He owed his life to this chap, and besides—he was *her* brother.

"Well?" said the older man impatiently.

Very quietly Hudson told him of the sequence of events bearing on the jeweled ibis that had occurred since the night he aided Marian in Alexandria; of the death of Toni and Captain Cullen's threats; of Miss Chandler's peculiar action, and the murderous attack of the dress-suited *shenzi*.

"I want to thank you for saving me from that fellow," Dave finished. "I recognized you by the light of the street lamps, you know."

Chandler looked up with the nervous quickness Hudson had already begun to associate with him. "What do you mean?"

"I mean what I said. If it had not been for your quickness I would be lying on a slab in the morgue now. That fellow's knife wasn't a foot from my throat when you struck him down."

"I? You're insane, man. I haven't been out of this room to-day."

His voice was absolutely sincere. Certainly the millionaire did not have the appearance of a man who was lying, yet Dave was positive he had made no mistake. Chandler's face was not of an easily forgotten type. Yet there could be no logical reason for this fellow's denying a deed that redounded so greatly to his credit. The man was not lying. His eyes were frank and his tone positive. Dave admitted grudgingly that he might have a double, but the odds against two men with duplicate features being mixed up in the affair were enormous.

"Go on," Chandler encouraged. "What else have you to say?"

The engineer shook his head in a puzzled way. "I'm stumped. There was no more doubt in my mind that the face was yours than there was that Miss Chandler gave me this trinket to deliver to you."

Drexel held out his hand. "Give it to me."

Dave dropped the ibis into his palm, not dreaming of the astounding events that would follow on the heels of that simple act. For a full minute after he had unwrapped the image Chandler stood motionless, staring at it. Then the pallor in his cheeks deepened to a dull, flat white, and the purple circles under his eyes stood out like livid bruises. His self-control vanished. His face writhed with a horror and anger he tried vainly to control.

"So you're one of them, eh?" he said thickly, but the heartbreak in his voice was pitiable. "Well, you will be rewarded now—suitably."

"What do you mean?"

Chandler flung the ibis on the table without answering, and Hudson picked it up. To his astonishment he saw it was not the same trinket the girl had given him. It was carved of the same black wood, but there was not a jewel on its surface from beak to claws!

A medley of street sound drifted up from Piccadilly, but they suggested nothing to Dave. He was dumfounded. There was absolutely nothing he could say. He stood staring at it in silence.

"You are a good actor," said Chandler tremulously, "but you cannot fool me. I can pretty nearly figure out what happened. You've stolen the real ibis and abducted my sister. Now you have come here to blackmail me. But it won't work, my man; it won't work. Tell me where Marian is, or by God——" He took a step backward and flung open a door. Three dark-skinned giants in barbarically splendid clothes stepped in, each one gripping a long, curved knife.

"An eye for an eye," the young man said. "Unless you tell me where Marian is hidden these men will kill you." Hudson knew he was bluffing, for his voice shook and his glance wavered. But his servants were hungering to kill. Their eyes gleamed like those of animals' at dusk, and a drool of saliva appeared at the corners of their mouths. Two of them were vicious-looking thugs, and the third——

Dave sprang forward with a sharp exclamation. "You, Imam, you know me. I saved you and your mistress in Alexandria. Remember the man who would have shot you had I not taken his pistol. Now is your chance to repay me. Tell this man who I am."

The fellah, who had the sharp, unswerving eyes of a hypnotist, looked at him blankly, and shook his head.

"He lies, this Yankee water-devil," said one of the servants. "Let us send him to his fathers, most noble effendim. One blow and he will cause you no more trouble."

That was a nice trap for a man to fall into. Dave had done his best to help a distressed woman—a girl whom he admired tremendously—and as a reward both her friends and enemies sought his life. It was absolutely inexplicable.

Hudson clenched his fists and prepared to make a fight. If his heart was beating faster than usual he did not let them know it. "Before you set your bullies to work, Mr. Chandler," he said, hoping for the other's aid, "let me tell you one or two things. It is true that I have spent a lot of time in Egypt, but I never heard of the priests of the Theban Zeus, or Sesostris' prophecy or that disappearing-ibis thing until I left the country. I don't know why Miss Chandler gave me that jewel or how it disappeared or where she is now. Probably the world won't miss me a whole lot, but this sort of gratitude flicks me on the raw. Go ahead, but I'll give them a little battle before they slit my throat."

Two of the barbarians crouched, and the mild-eyed one thrust his hand into his blouse. In imagination Dave could feel those blades in his flesh already. He braced himself for the expected assault, and his eyes did not waver. There was a tenseness in the atmosphere that spelled trouble.

Then a low, steady knocking sounded on the door.

Chandler swallowed his emotion, and asked huskily: "Who is there?"

"It is I—Marian," answered a soft voice.

The nearest sedentary people, whose lives run in the usual groove, can approach Hudson's feeling of relief is when the home-run hitter of a rival club strikes out with the bases full. Though he had presented an unconcerned face to death, the reaction found him dripping with cold sweat.

Chandler jumped toward the door with a half-strangled shout of joy. The brown rascals slipped their weapons away in some hidden holsters and drew up at attention. Except for Imam, they appeared to be disappointed at the tame ending of the affair. As for Hudson, he sat down in a chair and grinned and grinned like some weather-beaten gargoyle. He thought his troubles were about over.

Marian came in smiling, tremendously changed in attitude since she had talked with Dave in Spitalfields Garden. In her wide skirts and spats and chic little hat she was so sweet that she set the blood of the *Asian's* ex-engineer pumping at faster than its normal speed. Chandler swept her in his arms and kissed her violently. Hudson envied him his privilege.

When the millionaire's joy had subsided a bit he picked up the false ibis and held it out to Marian.

"This gentleman," he said, indicating Hudson with a nod of his well-shaped head, "claims to be the one who was of such great assistance to you in Alexandria. He told me a remarkable story of meeting you in Spitalfields Garden. He said that you intrusted the jeweled ibis, which we have sought so long, to his care, and instructed him to bring it to me. When I opened the package it contained this worthless imitation. Can you tell me anything that will clear this up?"

The girl turned her eyes on Hudson; those wonderful blue orbs that had spoken more eloquently than her lips under the blue skies of Egypt and the foggy haze of London town. She shook her head. "I don't see how I can, Drexel," she said quietly. "I've never seen him before!"

CHAPTER IV.
THE STORY OF THE IBIS.

BY this time Hudson was almost inured to surprise, and, except for a slight flattening of the muscles over his jaws, his expression did not change. But he *did* lean forward in his chair and stare grimly at Marian in an effort to fathom her reason for denying him, just as her brother and Imam had done.

At a signal from the girl, Chandler dismissed his servants. When they had gone Marian went swiftly across the room to the young engineer. There were tears on the fringes of her velvety lashes. "What became of the jeweled ibis?" she asked excitedly. "I trusted you, you know."

Hudson laughed, but there was no edge to his mirth. "You know me now, do you, Miss Chandler?"

"Of course. I denied you before the servants because two of them—El Melik and Abu-l-Kheyr—are owned body and soul by the priests of the Theban Zeus. But that is beside the question. Where is the ibis? Drexel said that a bogus one was substituted. Oh, if you only knew how much this means to us——"

"As Heaven is my judge, I don't know," said Hudson solemnly. "After you gave me the jewel I was attacked by a man who looked like a Nubian *shenzi*—probably one of those Theban priests you've mentioned. He would have killed me had not your

brother, or the living image of him, knocked him senseless. Mr. Chandler denies that he has been out of his room all day——"

"Neither *have* I," declared the other vehemently.

"Then a man who is Mr. Chandler's physical duplicate stole the genuine ibis and dropped this substitute in my pocket. It sounds ridiculous, but it is absolutely true. Do you believe me?"

Marian essayed a wan little smile. "Of course I believe you," she assured him. "I said I trusted you, and I meant it. We want you to help us. Will you?"

"Will I?" cried Dave, and there was a vibrant something in his voice that brought a delicate color into Marian's cheeks. "Sure!"

"Good!" The girl drew up a chair and sat down beside him. "Then, so we may understand each other thoroughly, you must know our story from beginning to end."

"I would like to know how you found me in Spitalfields Garden."

"There is no mystery in that. Ever since you helped me in Alexandria I have thought of you—as a help to my brother and me," she added hastily as a warm light sprang into Hudson's eyes. "We have a wireless on our yacht, the *Sleeping Beauty*, and through it we found out when your ship was due in London. He added that we could not get a braver, straighter man in the whole empire."

The engineer shifted uneasily in his seat. A eulogy from Marian's lips was doubly complimentary, but it embarrassed him.

"That I met you in the East End was only the luckiest of chances," she continued. "You see, we have been searching the world over for the jeweled ibis. To-day we learned that it was in the possession of a well-known Egyptologist in this city. I went to his home to purchase it. Drexel would have gone, but he is too well known to the priests of Zeus. He would have been trapped—perhaps killed—and the ibis stolen. I hoped to avoid that, of course. So I became the envoy. Mr. Malmsey, the Egyptologist, was not at all eager to sell. I pleaded. Finally he agreed to part with it for twenty thousand pounds——"

"Twenty thousand pounds!" gasped Dave Hudson, who had not dreamed that the relic possessed such enormous value.

"Exactly that. When I left Malmsey's residence I was followed. You have no idea how utterly alone and helpless I felt. Busy London and the deserted desert was all one to those brutes in carrying out their purpose. In a flash it occurred to me that the *Asian* must be in port. I hired a four-wheeler, but long before I reached the docks that wretched Egyptian stopped my cab. I jumped out and ran away. Then I saw you—and you know the rest."

"Let me add an apology to my sister's explanation," said Chandler, with a care-worn smile. "I am very sorry that I threatened you, but you can understand how I felt. Those men are devils incarnate. Life means nothing to them, and when I thought of Marian in their hands——" He shuddered.

Hudson wanted to ask why they were risking their lives for an object like the ibis, but reticence prevented. It was their business, not his. But he was glad that he would be near Marian when danger threatened again.

The girl laid her slim fingers on his arm, as though she had sensed his thoughts. A thrill ran up Dave's spine. He wanted to fight for her, to stand between her and the brutes who thought a bit of wood and glass was of more value than her warm body.

"Why did that servant—Imam, I think you call him —deny that he had seen me before? Do you trust him?"

"Trust Imam? Of course. It was he who warned me that El Melik and Abu-l-Kheyr are agents of the priests of Zeus. He was deceiving them when he denied knowledge of you."

Hudson nodded.

As Marian commenced the fascinating story of the jeweled ibis, Dave laid back in his chair with his eyes closed, a slight concession to his weariness. For the first time Chandler had an opportunity of studying the engineer's physical characteristics. Nature had built him with an unsparing hand. He was well over the six-foot mark, and his frame was muscularly in proportion. There was nothing bulky about him. His was the strength rather of the panther than the lion. His face was striking enough to attract attention anywhere. Every feature expressed strength as vividly as his body, and a certain devil-may-care recklessness as well. There were tiny sprays of wrinkles at the corners of his eyes and lips that testified to many a hearty laugh. He was a fighter, but a good-natured one. As for his hair, it had once been brown probably, but it was so crisped by the tropic sun that it had faded to a nondescript straw.

Utterly unconscious that every point was being carefully catalogued, Dave listened to Marian's story, careful not to miss a single point. All of the places and a few of the names she mentioned were familiar, for Hudson's knowledge of Egyptian history was not quite as comprehensive as his acquaintance with its topography. The tale thrilled him. Though improbable to the verge of fantasy, somehow or other it impressed him as possessing a large element of truth. Such a belief could not stand the acid test of logic perhaps, but these young people had enough faith in it to risk their lives in the venture.

It had its inception during the reign of Egypt's warrior king, Sesostris, a thousand years and more before the coming of Christ. This mighty emperor conquered the peoples of most of the known world and added them to his tributaries. When he crushed Thebes, the Theban priests of Zeus invoked a curse upon him, and in revenge Sesostris abolished their order and sentenced them to perpetual exile.

In addition he carried off the two virgins who guarded the sacred fires. One of them he sold to the Hellenes as a slave, and the other would have suffered the same fate but for a vision that came to the king. In this dream a black dove warned him that if the virgin was sent out of Egypt it would cause the ruin of the empire, and it urged that, in order to propitiate Zeus, the girl be appointed as the country's prophetess.

In the first year of his reign Sesostris had commenced the construction of a pyramid on a plateau in the plateau region—a pyramid even larger than the wonder designed by Cheops. It was made of Ethiopian stone, and beneath it he builded a labyrinth, whose tortured twistings and turnings would—had

they been straightened in a single line—have extended more than a hundred miles. On this stupendous task fifty myriads of men were employed for a score of years.

By the time it was finished the Theban prophetess had grown into a woman of such intellect and beauty that Sesostris coveted her. She refused his advances, having dedicated herself to the gods, and the king pretended to take her answer in good grace. Instead, he flew into a terrible rage, and determined on revenge. His most wonderful chemist and necromancer, aided by the royal embalmer, had discovered a fluid that would suspend all the functions of living for an indefinite period or until a reagent was injected into the inanimate body.

This, then, was the punishment Sesostris designed for his beautiful prophetess. When she had drunk the potion he intended placing her in a room in the center of the labyrinth, and there she should lie, neither living nor dead, until the world crumbled and the stars winked into oblivion. It was a revenge worthy of the man who inspired it.

In this room Sesostris erected an altar. Before it he placed a couch in the form of a sacred bull, with incense burning at head and feet. The room he carpeted with jewels; the walls and ceiling he studded with the most precious stones in all Egypt. In fact, he had combed his tributaries for the richest offerings to do her honor. Then, as her unconscious body was placed there, it is said he relented because of her beauty. The revivifying fluid was hidden in the tiny hollow image of the sacred ibis, together with a plan of the labyrinth traced on a bit of papyrus. He started to open it, but was struck down by a servant who was in the pay of the priests of Zeus. The frightened slaves sealed up the room, and there the dead king and the senseless girl had lain while thirty centuries were born and died.

That was the story Professor Chandler—their father —had heard one night under the coldly glittering stars at Sa-el-Hagar. At first he scoffed at it as a fairy tale, but the teller had proof of his tale. He brought a papyrus, describing the pyramid and its secret. It had been secreted by the Egyptian's family for hundreds of years through fear of the priests of Theban Zeus. That vindicative order, which kept in existence in spite of its exile, always nourished a belief that one of their prophetesses would again guard the sacred fires. They believed that the body of the one Sesostris had coveted was hidden within the pyramid, for even tradition had forgotten the labyrinth beneath it.

Professor Chandler immediately became an enthusiast on the subject. If he could find the fluid that would bring the priestess back to consciousness he believed he would gain knowledge that would make him the most famous Egyptologist of his time. The jewels that were supposed to be hidden in the sepulchral chamber meant nothing to him.

The search for the ibis required an incredible amount of patience and a vast amount of money. Then it was merely by chance that he found himself on the trail of the jewel. Through all of his exertions he had been aided by his son and daughter, who were almost as anxious for success as the old pedagogue himself. When the elder Chandler died they pursued the search with undiminished vigor. So, at last, they had located the ibis in the possession of the collector Malmsey.

Drexel Chandler, who paced up and down the room while his sister recounted their adventures, paused in front of Hudson. The light of martyrdom flamed in his eyes. "The value of the discovery we seek is incalculable. We can learn much from the past, but we know little of it. Science, history, letters would all be benefited by the Theban priestess, and they shall have her knowledge if we pay for it with our lives."

Dave nodded. "That's all very well, but apparently you're just as far away from it now as when you started your search." He spoke to Chandler, but he looked at Marian. There were tears in the girl's eyes, and of a sudden her brave repression broke down.

"Oh, it means so much to us," she sobbed. "We felt so sure—and n-now it's all spoiled."

The engineer patted her heaving shoulders. "Don't do that," he blurted. "We'll get that cursed ibis back if we have to shake London like a tablecloth to do it. There was only one man who came near enough me to get it, and that was the chap who bludgeoned my assailant in Spitalfields Garden. It ought not be so terribly hard to locate him. All we need is a little speed and intelligence."

Chandler sprang up with sudden, feverish energy, and flung off his dressing gown. "You've given me new hope, Hudson," he cried. "We'll get that man, or——" He thrust his hand into his coat pocket. An incredulous expression came into his face, and he uttered an exclamation in a thin, astounded voice.

"What is the matter, dear?" asked Marian, startled.

Chandler drew something out of his pocket, and held it toward them. It was the jeweled ibis!

CHAPTER V.

MISSING.

FOR several hours after Marian and Hudson had retired to their respective rooms, Chandler sat by the window, brooding. He had been glancing over a copy of the staid London *Times*, though only one item focused his wandering thoughts. That was an offered reward of ten thousand pounds by the war office for the apprehension of the deserter whom Hudson had helped pursue across the Libyan Desert. The item told of the little expedition's fate, and incidentally praised Dave for his actions. Chandler smiled. It was evident that their new ally was a hard man to keep down.

Even that article bored him at last. He tossed the paper on the floor and walked to the window.

Opposite towered the darkened bulk of the Berkley. Beyond stretched the waste of London, presenting only a wet, disagreeable vista of roofs. Save for a taxicab rattling through the fog, Piccadilly was deserted. Empty as the monstrous city seemed, there were men out there who were eager for his life. Though Chandler was unemotional, and a chap with more than the average amount of courage, he shivered when he thought of the cold devilishness of the priests of the Theban Zeus. He feared for Marian—not for himself.

The mysterious loss and reappearance of the jeweled ibis puzzled him. Though he examined the situation from every angle of his experience, he could come to no logical conclusion. He had not been out of the room all day, and neither Dave nor Marian do such a thing as a joke. Besides, they had been as astonished as he. There was a reason, a sound, substantial one. Whatever it was, he intended to find it out.

His life during the past year had been like a bad dream. It was a wild chase after a will-o'-the-wisp; a pursuit, with desperate men, in turn, pursuing them. It was characteristic of Chandler that he never thought of giving up. The acquisition of invaluable jewels—except for their scientific value—meant nothing to him. Fame he did not crave. He was the cold, exacting scientist, but the most emotional of men would not sacrifice all for their profession as readily as he.

So little did Chandler care for any possible profits that might accrue from the trip that he had promised Hudson half of whatever they might find. The latter protested at first, but the millionaire pointed out that such an arrangement was absolutely fair. He was unacquainted with desert travel, and without a battle-ripened comrade they were almost certainly doomed to disaster. Certainly his services would be as valuable as Chandler's backing.

If the millionaire had known how badly Dave wanted money—not for itself, but because it would give him a fighting chance to win Marian—he would have understood the latter's exultation. As it was, he wondered if there was not a grasping streak in the weather-bronzed young wanderer. He hoped not, for Hudson was a man clean through.

As he paced up and down petty incidents harassed him—the insolent faces of El Melik and Abu-l-Kheyr when he dismissed them; the mild, curiously straining eyes of Imam; the determined way his father waved his gold-rimmed spectacle when he spoke of Sesostris' secret; the snorting of camels that woke him under the cold stars at Sa-el-Hagar.

How he wished that the whole blasted affair was settled; that he was back in New York with proofs of his work! Ardent scientist that he was, the laboratory appealed to him more than this search to prove an old necromancer's fluid of life. Not for an instant did he doubt that he would succeed, but there was Marian to think of. Adventure was all right, but not where she was concerned.

His nerves finally drove him into motion, and he walked up and down the room, tearing a cigarette to shreds between his teeth.

Matters were all arranged. His yacht, now lying in the Thames, had been ordered ready for departure at a moment's notice. They were to leave at six in the morning. Chandler was very glad that Dave Hudson was going with them. Manlike, he attributed the latter's willingness to a spirit of adventure, and not to the real cause, which was Marian. In their few hours of acquaintance Chandler had developed an enormous liking for the big, broad-shouldered engineer. Somehow his spine felt stiffer now that Hudson was here.

A sudden thought struck him. So many curious things had happened that it was quite possible the priests of Zeus had learned of their newly laid plans to board the yacht at six. If they had, there was bound to be trouble. Why not fool them by quitting the hotel now? He looked at his watch. It was two o'clock. By George, he'd do it!

He roused Marian by knocking gently on her door, and explained the situation through the keyhole. While the girl was dressing and stuffing a few belongings into a bag, Chandler awakened Hudson, and then called up the night clerk.

"I ordered a touring car for five o'clock, you'll remember," he said briefly. "I have changed my mind. Have the garage people send it around immediately."

There was a hint of astonishment in the clerk's voice, but he answered: "Very good, sir. Anything else?"

"You will see to it that no one other than the chauffeur knows of our departure. This is very important."

"Yes, sir. Thank you, sir."

Fifteen minutes later they descended in the lift, passed the sleepy but dignified porter at the door, and climbed into the tonneau of the big machine. A chilly wind was blowing the fog toward the river, and Marian, snuggled in her furs, lay sleepily against Chandler's shoulder. Hudson, alert for all his weariness, kept one hand on the jeweled ibis and the other on an automatic. He didn't intend to lose it again.

Nothing happened. The big machine sped through streets alternately gorgeous or sodden with poverty, but all veiled in the darkness. To Chandler London always seemed to be choking in its own vile air, and even the thought of getting away was exhilarating. Besides, Hudson had told him that there were no vessels in port that might be reasonably expected to follow them—except Captain Cullen's lumbering *Asian*—and that relic of the past was too slow to make a race. Now that they were safely off on the first leg of the journey to Sesostris' pyramid, with the ibis safe in Hudson's pocket, the haunting feeling of suspense departed from Chandler. With a start of a day or so he was sure of outstripping his enemies. As for the priests of Zeus waiting for them in Egypt, it was time enough to worry when they sighted land.

A launch waited at the wharf. It carried them over the dank, smelly water to the *Sleeping Beauty*, a lean, racy, one-hundred-and-fifty-foot yacht. The instant they set foot on board the engines began their monotonous clank. By this time Marian was almost asleep on her feet, and Drexel half carried her slim form to the stateroom and consigned her to the services of a maid. Chandler went direct to his cabin, and with a sigh of relief turned in. The deep purr of the machinery and the swish of water against the bow brought a sudden sense of freedom to him. His enemies were behind. The great spread of the Atlantic was before him. For a time at least he was free of care. So, musing, he fell asleep.

Had he been left to himself he would probably have slept the clock around, for, with the relaxing of tension, his exhausted nerves cried for rest. So the lovely dawn and the patter of feet over his head and any of the thousand-and-one sounds of shipboard were unable to wake him.

About four bells—ten o'clock—a steward pushed open the door and edged in sidewise. He was a peculiar-looking fellow, with a squash nose and slobbering lips. He wore an ugly, fixed grin, and spoke with a thick, cockney dialect.

"Will ye tyke yer bre'kfast 'ere or in the saloon, sir?" he asked.

Chandler sat up, rubbing his eyes. The sun flooded in through the porthole, and as far as he could see through the circular bit of glass was the laughing silver-blue of the sea. He stretched his arms and yawned. Then he looked more closely at the steward. The fellow was certainly an unpleasant-looking beast. Captain Gary had a habit of engaging men he knew nothing about, and probably this was one of his "pick-ups."

Yawning again, Chandler sat up and swung his legs over the side of the bunk. "I'll eat in the saloon, of course. Is Miss Chandler or Mr. Hudson up yet?"

"Not Miss Chandler, sir. Mr. 'Udson was on deck about 'arf an 'our ago, sir."

"Ask him to come here."

"Thanky, sir."

Whistling cheerfully, the millionaire bathed, shaved, and dressed. Still neither Hudson or the steward appeared. Rather impatiently he rang the bell. After an appreciable delay the cockney appeared. There was something in his attitude that reminded Chandler rather unpleasantly of a cat playing with a mouse. He grinned evilly and shuffled his feet.

"Well," said Chandler sharply. "I'm not accustomed to this sort of conduct from men in my service. Did you do as I told you?"

"Regarding Mr. 'Udson, sir?"

"Of course." The fellow seemed remarkably stupid. Drexel decided to speak to the captain about it. "By the way, you are a stranger to me. What is your name, my man?"

"Duffy, sir."

"Well, Duffy, I would like you to tell me exactly why you have not asked Mr. Hudson to come here. Speak up. Why?"

"Because 'e ayn't to be 'ad, sir."

"Not to be had," repeated the American, a sudden coldness striking his heart. "What do you mean?"

The steward's thick lips curled into a sneer. "We've 'unted the bloomin' ship from stem to stern for Mr. 'Udson, and not a tryce of 'im can we find. Mihap 'e's gone over the side. There's many a cove's done it who looked a bleedin' less despondent than 'im, sir."

"Gone," said Chandler blankly.

"Quite," nodded Duffy, with an evil grin.

CHAPTER VI.
THE CLASH.

CHANDLER scented treachery. It was quite possible that agents of the priests of Zeus or some of Cullen's thugs were among his crew, for Captain Gary was easy to deceive. If that was the case, they had doubtless made away with the big engineer. Drexel's feelings were akin to those of a man tied to a keg of dynamite with the fuse already ignited. Though the explosion was bound to hurt, it was preferable to the suspense.

The millionaire felt the hopelessness of the situation, but he searched the ship with the help of Imam.

As he expected, it brought no results. When he went back to his cabin he found Marian, white-faced and shaking, waiting for him.

"Oh, Drexel," she panted, "El Melik and Abu-l-Kheyr and the Egyptian who tried to kill Mr. Hudson in Spitalfields Garden are on board. Something must be done."

Her brother betrayed no surprise, but laughed mirthlessly. "Good Lord, what a stew, what a stew!" Then his face hardened. He drew out his revolver and spun the cylinder.

"What are you going to do?" Marian asked uneasily.

"Do? I'll show them. They won't get us as easily as they did Hudson. That's all."

"Hudson? What do you mean? What have they done to him?"

"He has disappeared. They've knifed him or tossed him overboard. There is no use hiding the seriousness of the situation from you. We'll have to face whatever comes——"

The girl sank into a chair and covered her face with her hands. The lace on her breast trembled convulsively. A tear crept between her clenched fingers, winking and sparkling before it fell.

Chandler patted her shoulder awkwardly. "Cheer up, little sister. It's a bad scrape, but we will weather it yet."

"Us!" she said passionately. "I was not crying because of our danger, but for Hudson. He was so generous in his sympathies, so ready to serve, and now—— Oh, are you sure he is dead, Drexel, are you sure?"

The man did not answer. He understood for the first time how his sister felt toward the big, good-looking engineer. Propinquity had bred—if not love, some emotion perilously close to it.

The rest of the voyage was a nightmare. Marian kept to her stateroom, and when Chandler walked the deck he did so with one hand on his revolver and a goosefleshy feeling that somebody was going to plunge a knife into his back. He grew pale and haggard with loss of sleep. His nerves, stretched to the breaking point, gave evidence in red-rimmed eyes and shaking hands. Shadows made him jump. The shrilling of the whistle startled him.

The sense of utter helplessness was galling. He spoke to Captain Gary concerning the men Marian had seen, but the self-satisfied old fool laughed tolerantly and told them every man in the crew was trustworthy. As the time passed Chandler began to understand that, if their enemies had killed Hudson, they had failed to find the jeweled ibis and that he and his sister were being spared to force them to reveal its hiding-place.

It was impossible, of course, for the suspense to endure forever. When they were but a day off Ras Alem Rum the cockney steward appeared in Chandler's cabin with his evil little smile.

"If it pleases you, sir, an' miss, some gentlemen would like to 'ave the pleasure of your company in Captain Gary's cabin," he said. Though the words were respectful, his tone was not.

"Did Captain Gary send you?" the millionaire demanded.

"No, sir." He had thrown off the mask completely now. "Some other gentlemen as would like to 'ave some bizness dealings with you."

The moment had come. Knowing that it would merely accentuate the trouble to refuse, Chandler and Marian complied with the impudent request. Though there was no color in her cheeks, the girl kept a desperate smile on her lips. Drexel was frowning, but there was fear in his heart when he looked at his sister.

A grim gathering sat around the desk in Gary's cabin. The captain, wide-eyed and bewildered, was tied to a chair. His partly bald head rolled from side to side in an effort to catch everything that was going on.

The man who had attacked Hudson in Spitalfields Garden appeared to be the leader. His flat, almost negroid features and fierce yellow eyes presented a remarkable contrast to his fashionable European clothes. He rose, with a bow to Marian, and commenced speaking in a soft, accentless voice.

"The purpose of this gathering," he said, "is, perhaps, not altogether unknown to you, nor are its members strangers. Your two ex-servants here—El Melik and Abu-l-Kheyr—are mighty pillars in the temple of Zeus, and enemies of the Muslim might in Egypt. The gentleman at your elbow there"—he indicated the smirking steward—"is Captain Cullen, of the steamship *Asian*——"

Cullen, the murderous filibuster, against whom Hudson had warned them! Chandler bit his lower lip to steady it. The lines were being drawn tighter.

"Last of all, I have the honor to introduce myself, Se-hotep-ab-Ra, a lineal descendant of the Theban dynasty and high priest in the order of Zeus——"

"You Nubian dog!" broke in Captain Gary, who had more courage than judgment. "I'll have you hung for mutiny when we reach Egypt. A descendant of kings, eh? Bah!"

Ra did not even turn around. "Throw him overboard," he said in a passionless voice. They dragged him up the hatchway, with the valiant old seaman barking defiance of them at every step. Above, they heard a hint of a struggle and then a splash. Some one laughed.

Marian shrank back, covering her face with her hands.

"You know what we want," continued the high priest. "The jeweled ibis is the sum and substance of our quest. I will acknowledge that you have outwitted us so far, if that will give you any satisfaction. Give us the ibis, and we will change our course and land you at Alexandria. You, Mr. Chandler, are an enthusiastic scientist, but even you would hardly sacrifice your sister and yourself for the unattainable——"

"What if I told you that I did not know where the jeweled ibis is?" asked Chandler coldly.

Se-hotep-ab-Ra rose, his tawny eyes ablaze. "We will hang you, Chandler effendi, from the mast of this ship, and as for your sister"—he ran his tongue over his thick, sensual lips—"her I will sell into the harem of my friend, Mustafa Kashif. You have heard how the Greek slave girls are treated. Will you subject your sister to that living death?"

The world went red in front of Chandler's eyes. An excess of rage choked him. Every muscle in his body tensed, and he breathed in short, hoarse gasps. The horror of it had him by the throat. There was no way of averting it, for he did not know.

"What is your answer?"

Chandler balled up his fist and struck Ra between the eyes with all his strength. "This is my answer, you damned brute!" he shouted. "This, this, this!" And with each repetition he struck and struck again.

He made a remarkable battle of it before they subdued him. El Melik tried to use his knife, and had it wrenched from him and driven into his shoulder. Though not an extraordinarily muscular man, Drexel was mad with fear and hate. When they battered him down at last there was scarcely one of them without marks of his fists. Besides, Abu-l-Kheyr had a bullet in the ribs.

Chandler lay all day in his bunk so trussed up that he could scarcely move. He ached from head to foot, and he was sick to the soul of him at thought of Marian's danger. For her sake he would have given up a thousand such jewels, but it was probably at the bottom of the sea with the ill-fated Hudson. His raw nerves urged him to scream, to kick, but he clenched his teeth and fought the hysteria. The sun sank in a blaze of glory, and purple shadows filled the room. At last he relaxed into stupor.

TO BE CONCLUDED.

Write!

We want you to write to us—to write freely—just what you think of THE THRILL BOOK, for your criticism will be of the greatest help to us in our constant effort to make each issue of the magazine better than the one that has gone before. Write us exactly what you think. Every letter will receive our most serious consideration. We welcome every point of view. We are not afraid of any opinion. A magazine that does not stand on solid ground degenerates into pretty poor stuff. The more interest you take, the better we like it. The old saying, "Every knock is a boost" fits us to a nicety. We are supplying a long-felt need—our magazine will publish the kind of story that all other magazines have relegated to the scrap heap because of their fantastic, weird, and thrilling nature. The success of such a venture depends upon our "honorary editors," our readers. We want your ideas as well as our own. Let us try to make this a kind of short-story club, with THE THRILL BOOK as the official publication, where at last we will be able to read the sort of tale which all our lives we have been longing to read. Haven't you noticed the lack of weird and unusual stories in the average periodical? We have. THE THRILL BOOK is the result of our feeling about the matter so strongly that we couldn't contain ourselves any longer. It seemed strange to us that after Edgar Allen Poe, De Maupassant, Ambrose Bierce, O. Henry, Frank Norris and Rudyard Kipling made their reputations by the out-of-the-way story, no magazine came along and made the idea a fact, so that the reader could get the benefit of it for a reasonable price.

The Man Who Met Himself

By Donovan Bayley

MR. RICHARD PANTON, missing his wife more and more, poured out another, and, this time, really final glass of whisky, dispatched it to join its fellows, lit his candle, extinguished the sitting-room gas, saw that all the doors and windows were bolted, barred, and fastened, and went halfway upstairs toward bed.

His intention, of course, was to go the whole way; but this was not carried out, for one of his feet caught in the stair carpeting, or possibly in a loose stair rod, so that, holding tightly to the candlestick, he returned, mostly through the air, to the foot of the stairs, and, being arrived there, further downward motion was arrested by the impact of the back of his cranium upon the tiled hall.

As a result of that violent resolution of forces, he sustained a certain degree of concussion of the brain, and lay insensible, with the candle still upright, and, rather strangely, still burning. Mr. Panton thinks that it did not go out, and it is quite possible that it did not.

Panton came to at last with a jerk, and sat up, while the stairs and the hall door produced the time-worn illusion of going round when they really were not. He refused to believe them; they presently quieted down, and then he saw something else that he would have refused to believe had he been able, but he could not do anything but believe, in spite of the locked doors and the fastened windows.

Standing halfway up the stairs, looking meditatively at him, very gravely, was a perfectly naked man, who, though he had never seen him before, seemed inexplicably familiar to him. He sat staring at him, his hands palm down on the tiles, the candle on his lap, unable to say anything, so much did he wonder.

The other man, however, had evidently no such disability, for he spoke serenely, his eye on Mr. Panton.

"What an odd creature!" he said. "I wonder why he was chosen for me?"

"You!" said Panton. "You! Who are you?"

"Oh, don't you know? To a very great extent I'm —you; in fact, I'm all that's really essential of you."

"When did you escape?" Panton asked caustically.

"It was less an escape than an ejectment. It happened when you drank rather too much and fell downstairs."

"What on earth do you mean?"

"I don't; it's hardly an earthly matter. It involves a thing that the part of me you are doesn't understand, the inner psychology."

"Say it again, slowly."

"No; it wouldn't be any use. I never have done things that are of no use; that isn't what I'm for."

"You seem very mad."

"Reduced to the basic fact, that means you don't understand me. Of course, now I'm outside you, you don't possess the means of understanding me, because no one can understand his subliminal self."

"His what?"

"I'll try to put it simply. Do you remember that you've often been puzzled about something, puzzled to distraction, and then given it up and said, 'I'll sleep on it?'"

"Yes, I've done that."

"And the puzzle's been answered in the morning?"

"Quite true."

"Well, I'm that."

"That? What?"

"The intelligence which settled your problem for you while you slept. I never sleep, you know, but I'm often very glad when you do, for then you don't distract me with your futilities."

"Here, I say!"

"What do you say?"

"Oh, hang it!"

"Hang what?"

"I don't know."

"That is like you," said Mr. Panton's subliminal self. "You say things that mean nothing, just because you like the sound of them. Do you know how you've always seemed to me?"

"No."

"I'll tell you, now I've the chance. You're a spuffling absurdity. You've made me feel I was locked up inside a bumble bee. You buzz, and you get emotional; you're in and out of paddies, and there is nothing to you at all but arrant curiosity about unessentials."

"It's a bit thick, coming into my house, with no clothes on, to tell me off like this!"

"I've always been in your house. You think I'm absurd because I've no clothes on. Stand up. You can now. Then see which of us two is the most absurd."

Mr. Panton got to his feet shakily, and looked down at himself. His lounge coat came to his knees, his hands were somewhere inside the sleeves; he felt his collar round his ears, and his trousers, which had been a shade short, were in folds round his legs.

"Don't you think you look a little absurd?"

"My clothes have grown!"

"You argue wrongly; you have shrunk."

"I've shrunk? Then where's the rest of me gone?"

"I've taken half of us. Half of us is mine, you know. When I was ejected from your body, I had to materialize myself, and, since you were my partner in it, I've borrowed, possibly forever, though I don't know, half of your frame. That was quite fair, for I've always had as much right to it as you."

"Do you mean that?"

"When you are better acquainted with me you'll know I never say anything I do not mean. Evasion is not one of my functions, and I function perfectly normally. I'm afraid you'll miss me, but I shall always be here, so if you want advice—and you'll find you will—I'll give it to you. That's one of the things I'm for."

"Do you mean to say you're part of me, that I've suddenly become twins?"

"You always were twins; every man has two entities, the objective self and the subliminal self. You, the objective self, are the portion which concerns itself with futilities, like getting on in the world, outshining your neighbors, and all that sort of thing. I, the subliminal self, am that part of you whose business it is to concern itself with the things that matter. For instance, when you've wanted to do something rotten, I've shown you very clearly what a beast you were. If you remember, you called me conscience then, and snorted at me; but I can say this much good for you—you've nearly always done what I advised, and when you haven't I've made you very uncomfortable, haven't I?"

"You have."

"That's another of the things I'm for. By the way, I find I'm getting very cold."

"Oh, are you?"

"Yes. I'm going up to bed."

"Oh, are you?"

"I've said so. You'd better come, too?"

"And what bed do you think you're going to?"

"Our bed."

"Our bed!" Mr. Panton mocked.

"Yes. You're very slow to realize things."

"What things?"

"Well, this, for instance—that it's just as much my bed as yours."

"Oh, is it? We'll see about that!"

"Naturally. Why do you say needless things? I've often wondered. Of course, we shall see about it."

The naked figure turned away, and started to go upstairs. Mr. Panton threw the candlestick at it, and hit it on the thigh. The flame went out, but almost before it had done so the angry little man—for he was a little man now, a very little man—jumped agitatedly, feeling on his own thigh the sensation of a burn.

"That was very stupid of you. I've already explained to you—now, haven't I?—that you and I are one. If you'd used your reason you would have known that anything that hurt me must hurt you."

"Oh!" said Mr. Panton.

"That ought to have been obvious to you. You needn't tell me where the bedroom is. I know."

Apparently Mr. Panton sat at the foot of the stairs for some time, wondering what to do. This impossible person seemed to have come to stay. How could he be got rid of? Mr. Panton saw no way. For instance, what was there to prevent him from saying that he was himself? That is—it was very muddling —what was to prevent this newcomer from telling everybody that he was him? He looked so like him that nobody would know he was not him. It might end by him having him driven out of his own house, for he was obviously a very clever fellow, and much more likely to be able to persuade people that he was him than he himself was likely to be able to demonstrate that he was not himself, and if he could not persuade people that he was himself, while the other managed to make them believe that it was he who was, then what would he—Mr. Panton—do? Mr. Panton understood this. He followed it all, because he knew what he meant.

II.

THE outsider, looking at the thing from a detached point of view, would have had another doubt, and that doubt would have been whether the man without clothes, or the man with clothes, was the original Mr. Panton, for they were so utterly alike that there was absolutely no evidence by which to choose. Mr. Panton was certain that he was Mr. Panton, but the other was just as certain that he was as much Mr. Panton as Mr. Panton was, and had gone to his—his refers to both of them—bed on that assumption.

Panton was not troubling himself with these abstruse theories. What was blistering his mind was the problem of how to get his bed back and eject the repulsive person who had gone to it, not to sleep, but to be warm. He sat there, and he wished that his wife—good, sensible woman—were only at home to tell him what to do. Then he wished that she would never come home, for which of the two would she choose? Would she choose either?

Would she not say that men do not shrink and that, therefore, neither of the two was her husband, but that both were only extremely bad imitations? Against that was the fact that he could remind her with circumstantial details of ten thousand little intimate things in their lives together. But then, so, apparently, could this other fellow.

It was about now that Panton saw red, and rushed upstairs. His war cry was:

"Conscience oughtn't to come alive."

He charged into the bedroom.

"What are you excited about now?" the stranger said. "You get more and more inept."

Panton flew across to the bed.

"Get out of that, he said. "I'm going to stand no more."

He took him by the hair, and pulled it, and immediately felt as though a monkey were seated on his own head tugging at his scalp.

"Hang!" he said.

"You're apparently quite unteachable. When will you grasp that we're each other! Get into bed, and don't be a fool!"

"How long are you going to stay here?"

"I haven't the least idea. It wouldn't have happened if you hadn't fallen downstairs. You did it."

"Are you going to blame me for everything?"

"Well, it's always been necessary so far."

"But what on earth will my wife say if you don't go soon?"

"Does it much matter what our wife says?"

"But she won't know which is which! She'll take you for me!"

"Well, I am you."

"Confound you!"

"You've been trying to do that for a long time."

"Look here, old chap, you really must go and find your home."

"My home is where you are. We've never been separated yet, and I'm not going to begin now."

He got up from the bed, and went over to the looking-glass, holding the candle, which he took from Panton.

"Come and look," he said. "Now, which of us is which?"

"Heaven only knows."

"Then why not make the best of it?"

"It's no good. You'll have to go." He took him by the shoulder, and then turned suddenly over his own, for it seemed to him that he, too, had been suddenly grasped.

"You'll get used to that. Supposing you were in the city, and I fell over the coal bucket while I was filling it for our wife, you'd have just the same sensations. No doubt in time it won't startle you, though I dare say at first, till you get used to being in one place and feeling you're in another as well, you'll have some bad few minutes. It's rather a lot to pay, isn't it, for that last glass of whisky?"

"You don't mean all this, do you? It isn't really true, is it?"

"It's very difficult indeed to know what truth is. I'm just telling you my theory. You don't seem to remember it's just as startling for me as for you. Now, come to bed. Come along, there's nothing to be got by sitting up all night arguing, and I find cold a most distressing sensation."

Finally, because there really was nothing else to do, he did get into bed, but his sleep was broken, for again and again the stranger woke him up to ask him, apparently merely from philosophic curiosity, why he had done various things in their common past.

"You mustn't mind," he said, "but I've never had an opportunity of cross-examining you till now, because when your part of our brain was awake it was always so occupied with funny, unessential things that I never could get it to listen to my part. Why did

you think it worth while, for instance, to tell our wife——"

"She isn't our wife; she's my wife!"

"Do you mind leaving that to settle itself when she returns? Talking about that, you could very easily let her have another fiver to enjoy herself. She doesn't have such a good time with us, you know, and even now, on her holiday, she's got the children dragging after her. We'll send her another five dollars in the morning."

"Oh, will we?"

"Yes. I'll come to the bank with you, and see you do it."

"Look here, is it my money or yours?"

"It's ours. There's another thing. Before you can go back to business you'll have to order yourself some clothes, or buy some ready made, because you're half the size you used to be. Order a suit for me while you're about it. Our wife would find it most inconvenient if I had to stay in bed all day."

"I'll be shot if I do!"

"No, you won't. You'll be followed everywhere by your double in a blanket until you give in. I shan't mind, if you don't."

"This is merely absurd. I'm going to sleep."

"Yes, you need it."

But ten minutes later he wakened him again.

"Why do you tell so many lies?" he asked.

"I don't."

"But you do. You told our employer only three days ago that you had urgent private business to do when, as a matter of fact, you only wanted to see a professional billiard match. If you'd told him that he'd have let you go, because he's quite a decent sort, and he'd have respected you all the more of telling the truth. That's true, isn't it?"

"I suppose it is."

"Then why did you lie?"

"I don't know."

III.

THIS sort of thing went on all night, and in the morning Mr. Panton was feverish and weary. He felt hungry and not hungry at the same time. The not hungry was Panton (A) and the hungry was Panton (B). He went down to breakfast as soon as his ears told him that the charwoman had prepared it. Panton (B) went with him, wrapped in the eiderdown, and perfectly unembarrassed.

The charwoman looked round and saw them.

" 'Ere, you boys, who——"

She looked once more, screamed, rushed to the kitchen for her outdoor things, and ran down the street carrying them, firm in her resolution never to revisit that house, for she had no stomach for horrible duplications and shrinkings of respectable city men.

"Now see what you've done!"

The creature in the eiderdown looked at him patiently.

"If the woman had been philosophical enough to wait, I could have explained it to her."

"But she wasn't. You couldn't expect her to be, and now you've lost us a perfectly good charwoman, a real treasure, as my wife calls her."

"I will explain to our wife."

"You won't be here when she comes back."

"How difficult it is for the objective mind to accept a new situation without protest. Do look at it calmly. Suppose I left the house in this eiderdown, perfectly unfitted as I am, unable, indeed, to procure myself a livelihood or clothes. I should immediately be arrested. That's so, isn't it?"

"I suppose you would."

"And a number of unpleasant things would be done to me. Do you admit that?"

"Oh, yes."

"Surely you haven't forgotten that you'd feel them all, too?"

"Good heavens!"

"Well, wouldn't you?"

"Yes, I suppose so."

"You would. I'm a dreamy creature; my world's more or less a world of dreams. I should be nearly certain to get under a motor bus. Think what it would be like for you if I were lying in hospital with a broken back; and do, my good self, try to remember that it was your own action which caused this disruption. It's done, and you'll have to put up with it. You go about your business, my good soul, and adapt yourself to the new circumstances. Then I'll do all I can to help you. At present you stop me. Now, don't you?"

"Do you mean that this is going on forever?"

"No, not forever. It'll be all right when we die."

"Then I hope you die first."

"Oh, that was only figurative. As a matter of fact, you're the mortal part of us."

"Then perhaps you can tell me when I shall die?"

"No, I mustn't tell you that."

"You know, then?"

"Oh, yes, I know, nearly enough."

"Will it be soon?"

"My dear fellow, if it were another thousand years, that would only be the tiniest drop in eternity."

"Hum! Well, one thing's certain; I can't go to the office to-day. What shall I tell them?"

"Why, the truth."

"But, man alive, how can I?"

"My good fool, you'll have to. Don't you see that? When you go back, half your original size, don't you think they'll ask you questions? You can only tell them the truth."

"But they won't believe it. They'll think I'm lying."

"I know. As soon as they think that, they'll recognize you. They'll listen to what you have to say, and they'll come to the conclusion that it's quite like you, and about the best thing you've ever done, and they'll make up their mind that you simply don't mean to tell them whatever it is that's happened. They'll find you know the work, and I'm afraid they'll find, too, that without me with you you'll do their cheating for them without any scruples at all."

"You don't know what you're talking about," said Panton, growing less and less hungry as the other ate.

"Now go round to your tailor and order a couple of suits. Our measurements are the same."

Panton did not know what to do. He was extremely reluctant to accept the situation, because, from first to last, he had never believed in it, though he had such good evidence that it had arisen. Finally, of course, he did accept it, and the most compelling factor was that he felt all this other creature's sen-

sations. That, as any one can see made it quite impossible for him to throw him out. He must have suffered a great deal during this time.

For instance, he had no privacy at all; he had pretty plain indications that even his thoughts were not secret. Looked at reasonably, this should not have worried him, for, if the stranger's explanation of his advent was correct, they never, of course, had been.

He went out from time to time, leaving the other half of him at home, and it did not even get his meals for him. It seemed to lie about and philosophize.

Panton (A) dreaded going to work, and wrote to say that he was ill. He got what money he wanted by letter from his bank, and he shambled to a tailor whom he did not know to replace with ready-made ones the garments that no longer fitted him. He had to buy new collars, too, but he made his old shirts serve.

It must have been a singular life he led, if his account be true; and there is evidence that it was true. For example, there were his desperate visits to the doctor in the darkness of night, to see if he could do anything for him. But no doctor can restore a man's size; there is Scripture for that.

No amount of medical thought could add cubits to the length of Mr. Panton, so the situation really resolved itself into this—that he was shut up, tête-à-tête, with his own conscience, to wait until his wife should return, to choose between them, and fearfully afraid that the choice would not be favorable to him.

IV.

THE stranger—it is preferable to call him that—became more and more irritating, more and more critical, more and more assertive in his manner, and less and less inclined to do anything for himself. He would lie and think for hours, too absorbed to notice that he was hungry, which meant that Panton (A) had to eat for both of them, and never feel satisfied.

As the date of his wife's return grew nearer, he became more and more desperate, more and more urgent that the other should go.

"Something's got to be done," he said. "I don't care what it is, but something's got to be done. My wife will be back in three days now."

"Our wife."

"My wife."

"Our wife."

"Well, anyway, she'll be back in three days, and she's not to find you here. Haven't you any pity?"

"You shouldn't have fallen downstairs. What pleasure do you find in that ghastly habit?"

"What ghastly habit?"

"Smoking."

"That's why my cigarettes seem to have gone off, is it? Is there nothing human you like?"

"No, not very much."

"You're a curse. But come back to what we were talking about. I won't have you here when my wife comes back."

"Our wife. I'm longing to see her."

Panton seized his hat, and went into the hall. The other followed him.

"Put on your overcoat," he said. "I don't want another of those ghastly things you call a cold in the head through your stupidity. While you're gone I'll write some more letters for us. They'll be more truthful than our correspondents are accustomed to get."

"Whom are you going to write to?"

"I'm going to write to that man who knocked you down with his motor bicycle, and admit that it was quite your—our fault. It was, you know. You're only trying to blackmail him into paying damages to keep out of court. If you hadn't run into the road suddenly——"

"You'll do no such thing! He's good for fifty dollars. I'm going to buy my wife a fur coat with it."

"Our wife wouldn't wear a fur coat got so dishonestly."

"This is where this stops," Panton said desperately, snatching up a heavy stick. "You're going out of my house before my wife comes home, if I have to beat you to a pulp to make you."

"Our house, and our wife."

Panton hit him on the head with the stick, savagely, though, it must be remembered, he had only half his normal strength. He expected to feel the blow himself, and he did. He reeled with the pain of it, and sank into a chair, his head splitting. He looked to see what he had done. The other was stretched on the floor, very ghastly in appearance.

"Great heavens!" said Panton. "I've got a corpse to explain."

He had an odd sensation, also, as though he were choking and bursting. A moment later he tore off his collar, which was strangling him. The next thing he did was to get out of his clothes while he could. All the time he watched the body on the floor, though not very closely. When he had nothing on but his shirt he knelt down beside the corpse.

That is, he would have done if there had been one to kneel beside. There was not. There was only a heap of garments. Mr. Panton looked at himself, felt himself, and went upstairs.

He came down again, clad in one of his old suits, and it fitted him. He looked at the diminutive clothing on the floor, wondered how he would explain it to his wife, decided he would not, picked it up, found his spade, went into the garden, dug a hole with it—a deep one—carefully shaped not like a grave, and buried the two diminutive suits, with the stock of tiny collars.

Now, there is one thing to be remembered: the doctor and the doctor's servant, as well as several of the tradesmen, saw him when he was half the size he attained on growing up, and is again now. That is all I know.

The Twisted Tapers

From the Russian of Larrovitch

THE tapers cast their shadows everywhere,
Across her breast, her eyes, her mouth, her hair.

We are alone; each taper bends and drips
While I pour kisses on her still, soft lips.

The shadows flicker on the walls and floor,
Faint sounds of voices reach me past the door.

The tapers bend and drip, the voices go,
The hours pass deliberate and slow.

She was a lady of a high-born race . . .
The tapers bend and drip . . . I kiss her face.

Ah! now to kneel within this heavy gloom
Here buried living in miladi's tomb.

In the Shadows of Race

By J. Hampton Bishop

CHAPTER I.

THE JUNGLE'S NIGHT.

IF any of young Duncan Whiting's fashionable friends could have seen his varying expressions, they would have considered them very amusing. It is doubtful but that he would have so regarded them himself had he been in a position to regard them at all, but, as it was, they ran riot, shifting with kaleidoscope swiftness, as his thoughts so directed.

He was extremely tired, and the broad tree trunk against which his back rested seemed gifted with an enormous breadth and a smoothness of bark, to say nothing of the comfortable, almost caressing, hollow into which his body sank, that was most remarkable.

Nothing else mattered—much. Even the blisters on his feet—the excruciating torture of the last few hours! Who could believe so small a thing could so unnerve a man?—even they were—comfortable.

He laughed, half aloud, and looked across at a figure humped on a small canvas camp stool, busily poring over a pocket notebook. Now and then he saw a blue pencil move swiftly across a page of the book. Why wasn't the man resting? Did he never tire? Only an hour ago he had limped before him on the heavy swamp trail, weariness evident in every turn of his body, yet now—there he sat squinting over a half-completed map and making notes. *Notes!*

Young Whiting groaned, and essayed to hunch his aching back closer into the comfortable hollow. This finally accomplished to his satisfaction, he gave a sigh of pure contentment and went on with his observations.

Dusky figures busied themselves all around him. Apparently tireless hands drove tent pegs and struggled with flapping canvas, while others untied packs and coaxed stubborn camp fires of half-soaked marsh wood. Oh, it was all so familiar! Their shiny, naked bodies glistening in the glaring light of the tropic sun; the mumble of their monotonous jargon to one an-

other; and the odors—the noxious fumes from the putrefying matter all about them—he shuddered, despite the accompanying ache that racked his very soul.

To think they were ten months inland! Ten months of swamp and mountain and forest; ten months of niggers and tropic animals; in fact, ten months of hell! And for what? Civilization? Bah! The name in connection with this became a mockery. Why, this was the undertow of the world; the garbage can of creation; the place where the mighty Creator threw the chips from his workshop and forgot them, left them to sprout and grow voluntarily into whatever they would, or to lie and rot and become—oh, what might they not become!

"Fever got you again, old chap?"

The figure of the camp stool bent over him and ran brown, capable fingers along his hand to his wrist. How cool they were—and strong!

"Just a devilish little, eh? Don't think so much as yesterday, but I'll fix you up another capsule. We'll camp and rest as soon as we reach the clearing. This is sure an unusual stretch of swamp, but I think we're about through it. We must be."

He turned and addressed something in a native tongue to a small, woolly-headed negro, wholly naked, standing behind him. "He's a dandy body servant, Waddo," he said, again addressing Whiting. "Best I ever had. Quick to learn, and almost capable for a savage. Can put his hand on any of my belongings at a minute's notice."

In an incredible short time the slim, dark body of Waddo salaamed profoundly before his master and he spread a medicine kit on the ground before him. Whiting swallowed the pill and washed it down with a gulp of boiled mud water, struggling against the overwhelming nausea that accompanied it, and once more leaned wearily against his friendly tree, watching the rapid approach of the coming night.

In the tropics darkness follows the disappearance of the sun almost before one is aware of the change, and especially this is noticeable in the lower altitudes, where the vegetation is dense. While the swamps, as night deepens, become little less than reeking, sweltering masses of steam, wherein all vegetation and animal life are drenched in a perfect sea of dew.

In the tent, after the evening meal, protected, in a manner, from this deadly "night rain," Whiting and his companion consulted maps, studied latitudes and longitudes, located as nearly as possible the trail of the day just passed. It was uncertain—its location—terribly so. No man—white man—had ever seen it before probably, or ever would again. Swamps unending; unexpected mountain peaks; forests impassable because of their jungle growth; plains—plains—plains; while through it and around it and over it all was animal life in every conceivable state of existence; all menacing, all threatening, all declaring, in every phase of nature itself, war—war to every and all intruders upon its domain.

At least it seemed thus to Whiting. He glanced up abruptly from where his pencil had just traced a stream, newly found that day, and looked across the small table.

"Duncan Whiting, Virginian, U. S. A., private secretary and companion to the Honorable Burton McLaughlin, also of Virginia, U. S. A., hereby resigns his job and proposes to hike, as fast as existing circumstances warrant it, back to the good old U. S. A." He stopped speaking to laugh at the concern in the other's eyes.

"No, it's not the fever; that's better. But I mean it, Mack. I'm done. I'm sick in the first place, which doesn't matter—much, but mostly we're going somewhere, and we're going hard. But where? How you hold up and tramp, tramp, and coax and coerce those damned heathen out there I don't understand. It'll get you, Mack. It will. And what for? To what end? Glory? You don't know the word personally. Honor! You're too busy handing it around to be expecting any, while, if it's just research, surely in the last ten months you've seen enough to know all there is to know about these cursed animals and the land they live in."

As Whiting spoke a peculiar expression spread over McLaughlin's face—a something between disappointment and a surprised understanding, and, seeing this, Whiting continued slowly: "Come on back, old man. It's not that I'm sick; I'm not, in the true sense of the word. I'm a regular bull alligator when it comes to toughness, but it's the utter futility of going any farther. Why, it seems a million years since we left that trig little river steamer with her shining brass and copper back there somewhere on the other side of the world and began this tramp which has brought us every day deeper and deeper into this nightmare. And what we've lived through aside from personal discomforts! Think of it all, Mack! Think of it! No sane person would believe it or care to listen to it. How many would enjoy a description of a native chief's burial ceremony, do you think? You're an excellent imitator. You might, if we ever do get back, give an account of one. And don't forget the poor wives buried alive alongside of their most worthy lord. And while you're about it recount to them vividly how you stood by and looked on

helplessly while an infant was steamed to death because of some hellish sorcery or another."

Whiting paused and mopped his face. He also essayed a weak grin. "It has sure got on my nerves at last, and I thought I didn't have any."

McLaughlin lighted his pipe and sat in deep study. From time to time he looked across at Whiting's perturbed countenance, but essayed no remark or gave evidence otherwise that he even knew of his presence. He got up suddenly and began to pace back and forth between the table and the side of the tent. That he was deeply moved was a certainty, and Whiting, attributing the cause to his fierce outburst, was on the point of asking him to forget it and "dope out" another pill when McLaughlin turned and faced him with an air of great determination.

"I'm going to tell you a story, Dunk, one I should have told you, perhaps, even before I asked you to make this trip," he said in a low voice, "and after you've heard me through, if you still wish to turn back—I'll know I was meant to do this thing alone."

McLaughlin seated himself beside the small table and folded his arms across its top. His face was white, and his eyes shone with an unnatural brilliancy. "My father was always deeply interested in ethnology," he began shortly, "and gradually my mother, after her marriage to him, became interested in it also. He had time and money, both conducive to the pursuing of whims or hobbies, and he spent much time in research and study. My mother's brother, Doctor Schofield—you know him—lived with us, and he and my father finally gave all of their time to the question of race.

"My father held peculiar views on this subject, which, after a time, my uncle came to believe also. In contrast to the belief that through evolution a monkey has attained humanity, he believed that through some crink of nature, millions of years ago perhaps, the human being had, because of peculiar circumstances unknown to us, deteriorated to that phase of the brute creation. His exhaustive study had strengthened, and, in a way, verified this belief until the unexplored haunts of the animals themselves became the one spot in the world for both of them.

"Of course they went; it was the one link in their chain of evidence that needed confirmation, and there was no obstacle confronting them. My mother would have had it otherwise, I think, but she stood on the dock with myself—a sturdy little chap—beside her that bright summer morning over twenty-five years ago, and smiled a good-by to him as he sailed out of both of our lives forever. No, he never came back. Somewhere in this land of mysteries and wonders he gave up his youth and his life—and to no avail. He died, I think, without the chance to even investigate his theory.

"My uncle came home two years later—an old-young man—white-haired, deeply lined face, and so changed it was difficult to recognize him as the man he had once been. He had evidently been through great hardships, and seemed unsettled as to facts. Of but one thing he seemed certain: My father was dead; but how or when or where we could not get straight. And Schofield took no more interest in the study of race. From that time until now he positively refused to discuss it at all.

"But the memory of my father kept fresh in my mind, and when, after finishing school, I announced my intention of spending a year or so along the west coast of Africa, my uncle grew strangely agitated and offered great inducements if I would give up the idea. But the inclination was too strong, and I spent the two years studying the coast negroes, collecting data, gleaning habits and haunts and languages, and when I felt I was as competent as I could get from such a life I went home for generalities and—you.

"My uncle absolutely refused to tell me anything concerning his and my father's travels, nor could I get a really good excuse why he should take this attitude, so I did something which you will scarcely understand; I resorted to theft! You see, I felt positive Schofield must have kept some sort of record, and on the chance of this I stole the combination of his safe one night when I was stopping with him. I found an old notebook in which were the names of steamers and towns and byways and highways of their trip together. That book was as a voice from the dead to me. Time seemed to leap backward across the years and give my father back to me. I need hardly tell you that I spent the entire night copying it, word for word, mark for mark, sign for sign—much of it was in cipher—and replaced it before morning.

"My conscience did not reproach me; instead I experienced the most exultant satisfaction, as if a task long delayed had been accomplished. I can't explain this; I am not a thief. But in this undertaking there is, and always has been, a subtle, impelling force stronger than the very life within me that has urged me on. I know not to what purpose or end, but its existence I recognize and respect. Call it what you will, laugh at it if you like, but I know it for a powerful factor.

"The notebook, as I say, is a sort of conundrum. And, loath to consult an outsider, I have done what I could working alone. The figures, of course, are plain. I know from them we are probably nearing the edge of the border of their last territory, but as a great deal of the particulars are in cipher it is very difficult to attain any definite knowledge regarding it. However, from several meager descriptions plainly written out, I feel morally certain we are following nearly, if not quite, their old trail. Why my uncle should have resorted to hieroglyphics I don't know, but I have heard my mother say his intention had been to write a treatise on the physiology of the ape. So, you see, he may have wanted to protect the information he gathered, and took this way of doing so. But if his investigations ever came to anything, no one has ever heard of it.

"You see, he has become very eccentric as he has grown older. He has a brilliant mind even now, and is consulted in the medical world on the most baffling questions, yet behind it all is the man—the man himself—whom no one knows and of whom few, if any, besides myself know of the existence."

McLaughlin paused and stared fixedly at a seam in the tent's canvas. "I doubt if I can explain," he said finally, "but he lives there alone, except for the servants, in that enormous old hulk of a house, and is never so well pleased as when let entirely alone. Not from look or word did I reach this conclusion, but from an undercurrent indefinable—a subtle something as mysterious as it is elusive. My mother, in a way, has sensed this often, I am positive, but if she voices any opinion at all his peculiarities are attributed to living so long alone."

McLaughlin paused again and looked searchingly into the face of his companion. The steel in his eyes sent out tiny sparks; his face held a look inspired by a great determination that had been acquired through much mental travail. Then he spoke with almost a hint of raillery: "You think I'm nutty, Dunk; a clean down-and-outer, don't you? Well, I'm not. There's something back of this—something that has been waiting these twenty-five years for me—me. I feel it; I was never more sure of anything in my life and I'll never stop until I have unearthed it. What I have made a mistake in was to bring another white man in here, and, worst of all, to expect him to believe in what he must consider the product of a distorted imagination. I see the mistake now; but, oh! what's the use? We're here, and I'm going to stay. Also, I'm going on. If every damned negro mutinies I'll still go on. To me it is a tangible thing. I feel it. I know it. I know my father, young, vigorous, full of the joy of life, came in here and never came out again, and that his companion never gave any details explicit enough for my satisfaction. And the fact that he stayed two years alone in a country which has since been proven was extremely distasteful to him only adds greater evidence to the mystery. That's the end of the story. Not much of a story, perhaps, to the analytical; merely the egregious blunders of an egotist's wild imaginings, but, Dunk, it's a good old American hunch that I have possession of and one that has been steadily growing this long, long time."

For answer, when he had finished, Whiting reached his hand across the table, and McLaughlin took it in a good, strong grip.

"It was a corking story, old man, if a bit out of the ordinary, and I'll say just this: I'm with you to the end. There's a bare possibility the hunch may be contagious, and, anyway, you'll need help if, as you say, the natives should mutiny."

Outside the nocturnal chorus of the tropic night rose and fell, rose and fell monotonously, accented by the peculiar, penetrating whoof of the hippopotamus or the strident roar of a dissatisfied alligator for his mate, while two men sat through a long moment and—understood.

CHAPTER II.

LIKE AN APPARITION.

WHEN Whiting awoke the next morning, after a restless and uncomfortable night, he lay for a while looking through the dew-sagged netting of the tent's side into the impenetrable fog of the early morning. As he watched, the gray sheet of vapor changed imperceptibly from gray to softest mauve, then shifted to the faintest blush pink shot with violet rays, then back again to the monotonous soft gray to start all over again. He knew the bright sunshine back of it was the cause of all this, and he hoped, as sometimes occurred, the wind would come to the sun's assistance and clear the atmosphere before noon.

He heard the natives already busy coaxing the camp

fire and the thump of packs under experienced hands. He stretched out his legs and speculated as to their endurance should the swamp continue, and pressed his tongue tentatively against the roof of his mouth to see if the whang of the quinine was still there. It was. What was more, it was under his tongue this morning; his very breath was reeking with it. A self-respecting malarial germ must be a good one that would attack such quarters!

From somewhere through the mist came McLaughlin's voice, intermingled with that of Waddo. Already he was on the spot—a born general—encouraging, commanding, a note of actual cheerfulness permeating every accent. What a man! Lord, what a man! That his executive ability and abounding energy should be wasted on the managing of a common coast native! But no criticism, else—— Whiting, making a wry face, sat up and reached for his swamp waders.

It was almost noon when the fog suddenly cleared away and the clammy, penetrating atmosphere disappeared with it, followed almost immediately by a terrific heat, sickening in its intensity. Already the caravan had been on the march a good five hours and were feeling the effects of the tortuous trail. Far ahead, as cattle following each other on a footpath, native followed native—packs on head, the sun glistening on their bare, greasy skins as an armor—while the two white men followed after, unhampered save for their guns and the indispensable heavy clothing against the heat of the sun.

On either side rose gigantic papyrus whose roots were interspersed with mammoth ferns and "love-lies-a-bleeding," while here and there shone a gorgeous red-purple Dissotis flower or a pink or lavender-colored Pentas. Sages and mints of various species and scents also offered themselves for inspection, while in and out of this vegetation flitted peculiar types of bird life wonderfully colored in black, white, dove, and crimson.

All of this extravagant display was lost, however, under the more pressing demands of personal comfort. When they encountered their first swamp, Whiting and McLaughlin had stopped, enthralled, at the wonders of nature; but now—truly how we become beings of habit!

Toward the middle of the afternoon the inevitable hill, succeeding the swamp, was sighted. The porters quickened their steps, if such a thing were possible in the tiring muck, and McLaughlin turned an animated face to Whiting. "Grand luck! Thought we were sure in for it. Holy smoke, but the joints in my knees are there no more; just a meshwork of throbs and aches!" His voice held a boyish ring despite his admission. "Come on, Dunk, it's ours for the taking. Just look at those mallows—and the forest ahead; it's one big rose garden! I'll bet there's water there, too. *Water*, boy, how does that sound?"

Success to the human race is as invigorating as a draft of old wine, and the weary stragglers issued out of the swamp and up the ascent in a sudden rush of hilarity. As if expecting them, a sweet, cool spring gurgled its way across the moss at the foot of a homey-looking baobab tree, and offered a refreshing luxury after their days of unpalatable swamp water.

Because of the spring and the need of rest, they decided to make camp for a few days. And by eve-

ning the packs were barricaded a little farther back in the forest, with the two man tents put up at each end of the pile. These were so placed in case of attack from some hostile band of savages whose appearance they had so well learned to expect. They were far beyond the regular boundary of the explorer or the homes of the more civilized native bands, and might encounter anything.

Weird tales, fabulous in nature, had been recounted to them along their march by different tribes. It seemed that there was a mysterious land, vague in its whereabouts, that was ruled over by a daughter of the sun. Goddess of Fire was she, and beautiful— oh, most beautiful! But terrible beyond words. Even the wild beasts feared her and obeyed her, while man, if he but looked upon her face in the light of the sun, would be consumed by an unquenchable fire!

This remarkable land held further wonders. It was inhabited by a kind of man that couldn't talk, but possessed a wonderful strength which he used in behalf of this wonderful goddess, so that it was said her slaves—natives captured by these men—made a large colony. Her treatment of these slaves and her ability to retain or send out her deadly power at will only added elaborate touches to a legend whose veracity no native could doubt.

These stories, coupled with the thought that daily they were going farther away from all known haunts of men, had done much toward strengthening a disquieting attitude among the porters; but McLaughlin, through sheer force of will, had repeatedly overridden their superstitions and their fears, until he felt a tinge of pride in his success and almost a feeling of security.

It was patent in his every movement when, toward evening and fresh from a clear-water bath, he flung himself upon a grassy slope beside Whiting and lay looking around him. "Some country, Dunk, when a man's got the earth under his feet and isn't dying of thirst. Eh?"

Whiting, as if to verify his companion's assertion, lazily raised to one elbow and took in his surroundings —their packs and tents, the sprawling natives and the fiery ball that, a short while before, had been the sun. Across the jungle swamp, above the green, green rim of a distant cluster of tamarinds, the sun swayed triumphantly and threw a mellow, almost unearthly, glow over the waiting world. To the right, and far across the swamp, the satin-sheeny fronds of the graceful plantains glistened and shimmered and reflected the variegated glow of the forest wall to its rear. Here nature outshone herself. One caught glimpses of a deep crimson efflorescence intermingled with great, fluffy splotches of sulphur yellow, while the whole seemed overcast by a soft lilac white, as if a giant fairy had dropped, with careless hands, immense puffs of lavender snow.

Whiting sighed, and again lay flat. "It's sure there with the goods all right when it comes to colors. What the devil it's here for—all this wasted splendor —I can't see. Not for the 'crackers' which occasionally infest it, I'll swear. You know as well as I——"

Whiting paused and suddenly sat erect. His eyes actually bulged at what he saw. Over a rise in a small, open section appeared a queer sight. It was a procession. But what a procession! At the first look at it McLaughlin was on his feet, gun in hand.

Whiting followed him, a bit dazed, but the grotesque parade appeared not to be aware of their presence, though the camp was in plain sight. Instead, it turned slightly, angling to the right in the direction of the spring, and thus came in full view of the white men.

To the front and slightly in advance, as if to clear the way of all intruders, marched a heavily tattooed native—naked—while following, Indian file, was a conglomeration of blacks, long spears in hand, as varied as the numerous tribes from which they had undoubtedly been purloined or forced. In the center on a platform litter covered with soft fur and held aloft by a half dozen natives was the acme of this unusual party. An enormous leopard, his gaudy spots shimmering with iridescent brilliancy in the oblique rays of the sun, occupied the rear end of this litter, while well to the front was an—object, a thing that at first glance reminded the onlookers of some terrible freak of nature wherein the human had given way to some repulsive phase of the brute, culminating in a hideous creature neither man nor beast. Between these two, voluptuously reclining on the soft fur, was something at sight of which the native porters fell on their faces, crying aloud over and over, pitiful, beseeching pleas to their pagan gods, while the two white men breathed only in little gasps. It was a white woman!

Nonchalant, languid, she lay there as some dainty queen—an exotic human plant in a foreign world.

At the cries from the porters the party halted suddenly, and the men, looking, saw the woman leap to her feet and stand stock-still, observing them.

She was superb. Magnificently proportioned, yet gracefully feminine, she stood silhouetted against the olive green of the forest thicket. A mass of tawny-brown curls fell around her shoulders. She was clad in a white robe girdled in at the waist and reaching to her knees. Her throat and arms were bare.

How long she stood thus, looking, they never knew; but she turned finally, and apparently spoke, whereupon the column circled sharply, and in an incredibly short time disappeared through the wall of green underbrush at the rear.

McLaughlin and Whiting both stood staring blankly at the spot where the apparition had disappeared. It had been there. But it wasn't! It *couldn't* be!

McLaughlin came to himself first and attacked the moaning natives, who were still lying face to earth, with an energy most surprising. "Grand lot of protection you'd be," he stormed, in his excitement speaking in English. "Get up out o' this and change your cowardly hearts for a bunch of waste!"

"They'd probably get you sooner if you'd speak their U. S.," laughed Whiting, fairly doubling over in his mirth.

"I'm damned if I see the joke," barked McLaughlin as he administered kicks right and left.

"You don't now, Macky," cried Whiting with accumulative delight, "but you will. You will when you get my side of it. Egad! It took three days of swamp travel and the witchy draft of an equatorial magic spring to bring on this delusion of the imagination, but, boy, boy, it got your pep. Mine, too, perhaps. But I still retain enough unimpaired gray matter to appreciate the fact that you *can* lose that wonderful self-control of yours!"

But McLaughlin was addressing the cringing, shaking creatures in their own language now, his tone dominant, ringing with a note of power; a demonstration of a superior will over that of a lower caliber.

Whiting, finally sensing the gravity of the situation, joined his companion, and the two of them worked, promised, threatened, until a semblance of order was finally restored.

McLaughlin then clearly pointed out to them the necessity of being ready in case of attack, which did more for their self-control than any amount of promises or threats, and they immediately began preparations.

Night came down suddenly. A dark gray curtain, shifting into a purplish blue, then black, spread over the sky, and tiny points of light pushed their twinkling faces through the mesh and saw the little camp quiet and settled for the night.

The guns and ammunition were arranged in convenient piles, and water was ready in case of fire. The natives were sleeping soundly under the soothing influence of full stomachs and McLaughlin's assertion that he would keep guard. He and Whiting would take turns, but because of Whiting's battle with malaria he was to be given the first chance at sleep.

He seemed in no hurry to take advantage of this privilege, but sat in the shadows with McLaughlin and smoked. Both were strangely quiet, seemingly loath to break the silence, yet each knew the other was laboring under a heavy burden of thought. At last the irrepressible Whiting removed his pipe and burst out with a short laugh: "We didn't see anything, Mack, not really. You *know* we didn't. It's the effect of that cussed swamp water! That's enough to make a man see anything, while as for those fool niggers they are so keyed up with superstitions boiled into their systems for generations that a hallucination of yours or mine would be visible to them. Sort of a telepathic transposition of a chimera, I'd call it."

McLaughlin also removed his pipe, and sighed heavily. "She was white, Dunk," he said quite irrelevantly.

"Like a pretty ghost," corrected Whiting, holding to a levity he was far from feeling.

But the other would not be turned aside. "And that hellish dream creature—that gorilla thing on the litter with her. And that leopard! Dunk, I'm not a coward, but—well, I'll swear I felt ice water—here in the tropics—running through my legs where the blood ought to be! It's the impossibility of the thing; the unreasonableness of it. A leopard, a gorilla, and a white woman!"

He leaned his back against the tree trunk, and stared off into the murky blackness of the night.

Whiting shivered, then hated himself because of it, after which he gathered fresh courage from the thought of his self-abasement. "Well, for the love o' Mike, don't let that pipe go out," he fired truculently, "else it's me for the tent netting. Those swamp animals with wings have industrious noses, and they seem cheerful in their duties on me, if my hide is full of quinine."

But McLaughlin continued staring, and finally commanded Whiting to go to bed. "We've got to sleep some time, Dunk, and we can't trust those fool natives, unless its Mago or Yuema, and I want to save them.

Besides, they're full of this witch business now. No; I'll call you when I can't stay awake any longer."

And Whiting, who still carried fever, went thoughtfully to his tent, being careful as he raised the netting that no insects got past.

CHAPTER III.

IN THE FORESTS AHEAD.

McLAUGHLIN never could tell how long he had sat there, alone with his thoughts, when he sensed the feeling that he was no longer alone. He sat erect, and stared into the darkness about him, much as one does who feels invisible eyes upon him from behind. Not a sound, save the whine of some night insect, the occasional flap of a fruit bat, or a distant splash of a prowling jungle creature in the muddy depths of the swamp water. He cocked his ear and listened intently. He held his breath, and endeavored to still the throb, throb against his ear drums. He was getting nervous as a woman. He leaned again against the tree, disgusted with himself, and yielded suddenly to the utter weariness possessing him, that pervaded his entire body and thumped its admittance through the channels of his brain itself.

He was very tired. What if he couldn't understand? Perhaps to-morrow—in the broad light of day—— That swamp *was* a hell—a wet hell—and it was delicious—this rest. He half closed his eyes, and a light, airy sensation, such as accompanies the first sweet whiffs of an anæsthetic, swept over him, lulled him, drugged him literally and then carried him away, above the heavy darkness of the forest, across the stretches of hills and marshes and scattered native villages, across the rough waters of the intervening ocean to the very portals of home itself, and—he slept. Not heavily, but with occasional flashes of semiconsciousness, wherein he knew the necessity of keeping awake. But each time, before he could grasp the thought firmly enough, it evaded him and he was off again, within the twinkling of an eye, to that land which knows neither time nor space.

He dreamed lightly, a queer mixture of a troubled dream, wherein some woman was near—very near; in fact, her eyes were opposite his own and held a peculiar, penetrating brilliancy, while her breath—or was it her hair?—seemed inoculated with an overpowering odor of crushed flowers!

And then he opened his eyes and saw her, and at first he thought he was asleep. A white face, framed in a cluster of suspended curls, hung in space not two feet from his face, and, grotesque as was the thought, it was upside down! The eyes staring out from this queer apparition, even in the heavy shadows, were intense and possessed of an unusual brilliancy, penetrating through these shadows.

McLaughlin sat quite still and stared back—a sort of hypnotic influence impelling him; yet he knew, somehow, it was all very unreal. The white, bare shoulders and arms and the indistinct glimpses of a white robe disappearing in the depths of the foliage above—— It was a nightmare, the product of his tiresome days along the trail and the unreasonable ending to the day just passed.

Yet his eyes were accustomed to the darkness, and he looked hard. The face appeared real—wonderfully alive. He felt the soft touch of a breath on his face! He sensed again the too-sweet scent of crushed flowers, and a blinding, unreasonable rage swept over him. This devil creature, be she woman or beast or spirit, should haunt him no more. He would *know* about her!

He reached out suddenly, but sudden as was his motion hers was quicker. Without effort the body curled sharply inward, then upward, and, with what appeared to be one movement, disappeared from sight.

He sat and stared helplessly upward. The forest trees were thick here; it might be possible to climb from one interlocking limb to another, and thus, so on through the trees—if one were a good climber—and it were daylight; but at night, and a white woman! Good God! The thing savored of black magic. Of all the unreasonable, inexplicable phenomena he had encountered in this land that was the home of witchery and sorcery and superstitions, this ranked first. There must be some explanation. He was overtired, perhaps. His nerves—now. He got to his feet shakily and fairly staggered to Whiting's tent.

He lighted a candle and sat on his listener's feet while he talked. "It's witchery, Dunk; it must be. The *par excellence* of all Circean stuff under the sun —and to think we'd have to run into it!"

Whiting sat up on his skeleton-collapsible cot and shook a sleepy, touseled head. "And you say the lady hung head down, eh? Must be quite some acrobat. We'd best capture her, huh? Menageries, you know. Good money; fine investment. Unless there's danger of gettin' us under the spell. Bewitchin' us or somethin'." He cast a skeptical eye at McLaughlin, and then lay back and choked with unrestrained mirth.

"Um-m-m—— His lady-love comes a-wooin' at night and approaches him, head down, from the limb of a tree!" he chuckled. "What! Huh? Say, go home and tell that. But first you want to be prepared for substantial restraint the rest of your life, Mack; you'd never live it down."

McLaughlin's face was scarlet, but he laughed in spite of himself. "You blithering idiot, I'm tellin' the truth!" he yelled. "And I wasn't asleep, either. I'll admit I *had* been, but she—she—well, she woke me."

"Yeah, she did," sanctioned Whiting assuredly. "She must have. Merely clasped one toe around a twig, and, swaying jauntily in mid-air, suggested casually that you get back on your beat. Very simple, um-hum——"

"You go to the devil!" commanded McLaughlin as he started to leave the tent.

But Whiting sat up, hand over mouth. "Hold on, Mack," he gulped, "and don't hold that netting up, you chump. Come back here and sit down. Of course I believe you. But wake a man up out of a sound sleep to listen to a yarn like that! And expect him to believe it right off the bat! Holy smoke! You know it listens worse than the 'Arabian Nights.'"

McLaughlin came back and sat down resignedly. His sudden flare seemed to have disappeared. He was still, in a manner, dazed, however, and Whiting noticed the almost helpless look in his eyes. "Buck up, old man!" he cheered. "You know that ancient stuff about the faint heart and so on. This seems damned queer, but probably when we're on the inside track it'll be as easy as an old-time picture puzzle. The only thing——"

"You can believe it or not, Dunk," broke in McLaughlin, "but I tell you the thing was hanging head down, and it was alive! I felt the breath—and the perfume. I never smelled anything like it; thick so you could cut it with a knife, and sweet! Lord!"

But Whiting wasn't listening. Instead, he leaned forward and grasped McLaughlin's arm. His face was set; he was laboring under suppressed excitement. "Where is that book—the copy of that book you made?" he demanded roughly. "I'll bet we're on the track of the very thing you're looking for. Get it and see if we can figure out anything."

When McLaughlin returned with the book, Whiting was busy laying out maps and instruments in little heaps on the bed. He added a pencil and sketching pad to the list and sat down. McLaughlin also sat down, and they opened the book.

Whiting had never seen the book before, but whatever delicacy or hesitancy he may have felt concerning it was forgotten now in the pursuance of his big idea. Nervously he scanned the pages, consulting the maps whenever the figures were decipherable. McLaughlin, too, bent close, and, with pencil poised, located certain spots they had passed, referred to in the book. The pages in cipher they, perforce, skipped, but the written descriptions Whiting read aloud, hurriedly, feverishly, almost as if he knew the climax awaiting him.

A few sentences giving general directions here, a disconnected jumble of recorded camp trivialities on a little further, a half dozen pages on the habits of the natives still further on, and then a page over which he halted and bent thoughtful brows. It was toward the end of the book, recorded after the manner of a diary, and began quite abruptly:

"A three days' swamp to the back of us and the jungle forest ahead of us and our porters threatening to mutiny because we're nearing the land of the wild men! Poor, ignorant fools! But who knows? Perhaps they are wiser than we. I can afford to theorize, however, as we'll probably be here three or four days on account of the supply of spring water and Mack. He wants to wash some of the quinine out of his system with water that isn't filtered mud. Lord, but the taste of that water to-day—how we did drink of it!

"Killed a lion this morning. She came to the well to drink——" Here McLaughlin interrupted to say that the words had been written in pencil originally and were so marred he couldn't make them all out, thus accounting for the disconnected run of sentences. Whiting bowed and read on. "Mack has fever and is delirious part of the time. Ought to be getting on, but must wait until he is at least rid of the fever. He has swallowed enough quinine to do away with any malarial germs, but it still seems to hang.

"Explored the forest a bit to-day, and it appears to be almost impenetrable—overrun with an excessively rank vegetation. Thick underbrush and creeping plants between giant trees that shut out the sun except at midday, when thin pencils of rays penetrate into the gloom, promises a difficult hindrance to our further travel, unless an ancient path might acci-

dentally be found. From the location—somewhere between five and ten degrees N. and ten and twenty degrees E.—I think we must be near the home of the gorilla himself."

Here Whiting stopped, and again they bent over maps, faces alert, tense, betraying the eagerness they didn't try to conceal. McLaughlin pointed a convincing pencil to a spot on the map.

"We've hit it square, Dunk." His voice shook with an uncontrollable excitement. "I'm dead sure of the thing. Of course in this region of swamp and plains, to say nothing of the forests themselves, it's hard to be certain, but from his description and location —vague as it is—I feel that we're on the border all right. Right in here we should find them—the gorillas. It is their natural home generally, besides being perfectly adapted for them locally. They attain to the densest, darkest, gloomiest forest for homes—and hear what he says of the forests ahead of them? Oh, Lord, if we can only go on now!"

"We'll read on a little further," interrupted Whiting. "Perhaps he gives more details."

The next dozen pages were in cipher, and imperfect apparently, at that, as if the author had been at variance with his own convictions. Then a line or so disconnected and irrelevant to all that had gone before it: "My God! Why did he do it? I know it was the only way——"

Then, farther down, interspersed with line after line of cipher, was a paragraph incongruous, dense, wholly mystifying: "Crazy! Yes. There is no world but this, and never was! Much better to have died— oh, yes! Pain in leg is better—— Gone. Trees! Stagnant water! Ugh! And, Mack, you know now it was the only way, don't you? Yes? They've been kind—human—to me, Mack, and they thought you were an enemy! Forgive me, Mack. Life is sweet even here—even here, Mack, old man——"

Then cipher and more cipher. On the last page Whiting read with a touch of finality, as if he were responsible for all that had gone before: "I'm home, thank God, and it's more than I ever dared hope. My new book is open, with clean white leaves. May it be given me to forget the pages of this with the closing of its covers. Burton Schofield."

"'Take Me Down to Blinky, Winky, Chinatown,'" suddenly hummed Whiting; then: "Egad, it makes me feel like a sneak thief, a helpless fool, and a cross between a crazy man and a drunk all in one. On top of our entertaining day and your vivid sketch of your evening's entertainment, I feel that we must have somehow got hold of a liberal dose of hashish. But nevertheless, Mack, it's it! That white woman and those damned beasts, you'll find, are at the bottom of your hunch."

"But she's a young woman, Dunk," interposed McLaughlin almost petulantly. "She can't be as old as you or I. How the devil could she have anything to do with it?"

But Whiting's assurance was large; also he was very tired. He waved a hand. "Go and wake one of your trusties, Mack, and have him receive callers for the rest of the night, and let's get some sleep. To-morrow, when I'm not so cussed fagged, I'm goin' to unravel this. And don't forget," he called, "that the Goddess of Fire knows no age; she may have been as scrumptious a peach as this a thousand years ago!"

But the retreating footsteps never halted. Instead, a half-hearted "Oh, hell!" echoed from the direction of the native quarters.

CHAPTER IV.

BEYOND THE USUAL CHANNEL.

SOMETHING jerked Whiting to a sitting posture and then shook him—shook him till his head rolled from side to side, while he struggled painfully and suddenly from a very pleasant dream to the acute knowledge of McLaughlin's grip on the back of his neck. His eyes flew open, and he doubled his fists automatically. "What the—— G'wan out o' here! Can't you let a man sleep *none* of the time?"

McLaughlin's grip relaxed, and he stepped back breathlessly. "Yes, sleep, sleep!" he half snarled. "We've had too much of it now." Then suddenly: "Come here."

But Whiting lay back with his hands behind his head and yawned. "Lord, but this climate and Mack are a strenuous pair!" he complained to the universe. "It's me for the tall timber to sleep an uninterrupted week! I can't be scientific and live up to my high calling with my nerves on the ragged edge for a little sleep. Now, Mack——"

But McLaughlin raised the tent netting. "When you finish your monologue," he interrupted, "come out here and help me with these cannibals. Ten of 'em disappeared during the night, and the rest are worse than a bunch of tourists taking their first trip across."

He spoke calmly, and it took Whiting two full minutes, lying there and looking hard at the spot where McLaughlin had dropped the netting, to fully grasp the significance of. that last remark. When he did he almost knocked McLaughlin down in his headlong rush across the open way.

"When'd you find it out, Mack, and where the devil are they?" he demanded in one breath. He stopped and stared around wildly as if expecting them to pop out suddenly from behind a bush or a tree. "Suppose that hoodoo thing ran amuck and fed 'em to her pets during the night? Great Scott! What's that?"

McLaughlin almost smiled, if such a thing were possible under the circumstances, at Whiting's amazement. "That's the complemental return for the night's appropriation," he said briefly. "Seems our visitors have a semblance of honesty, if they are thieves, and this their idea of remittal."

It was a conspicuous heap near McLaughlin's tent and bore evidence of his recent investigation. The two men walked over to it, and McLaughlin, kneeling, invoiced the lot: Furs—rare ones—and elephant tusks, two of which were over six feet in length and would have made a tiresome load for two strong men; and fruit—bananas and pawpaws—and queer pots of tarnished, beaten gold filled with podocarpus berries and banana wine. McLaughlin looked up with a queer laugh.

"Took ten perfectly good porters and left enough stuff to make loads for double that many," he said simply. "Now what are we going to do?"

"That's simple," answered Whiting, who, with feet wide apart and hands deep in pockets stood staring down at the assortment. "We'll be strict vegetarians for a decade or so and give our porters one good drunk on this essence stuff here. They'll forget part of 'em's gone. Did they take our best ones?"

"That's the queer part. They seemed to choose promiscuously and worked evidently with no noise. Yuema, whom I left on guard, is gone, and Waddo." A tender, strange little smile flitted across McLaughlin's face at the mention of Waddo. "Yuema was of more value than the other nine," he continued softly, "but Waddo was human, if I did find him in this beastly country. Picked him up half starved and alone on the mole at Porto Novo one day over a year and a half ago, and he's been with me ever since. He's little and game." He halted and changed the subject hastily. "I've threatened death to the one who tries any stunts, but they expect total annihilation from some mysterious source anyhow, so my threat carries significance only while I have my eye on them."

Things indeed were looking serious. Whiting took a thorough inventory of the predominating mental temperatures of the remaining porters, while McLaughlin engaged one of the least affected in the preparation of breakfast. Whiting realized the futility of testing his influence if McLaughlin had resorted to force, but counterbalancing his friend's stolid, bulldog determination was his own great faculty for climbing, always unexpectedly and unconsciously, to meet an emergency, and he now so climbed.

A great, a stupendous, idea had come to him, and was instantly put into effect, the result of which he confided in his inimitable manner over their late breakfast. He spoke in a semiwhisper, as if confined within crowded quarters and there was grave danger of being overheard. But there was a devil-may-care look in his bright brown eyes for all his caution.

"Safe?" he bridled, at the tone of doubt in Mc-Laughlin's voice. "Wait. The thought occurred to me that the only way to fight the devil is to use his own weapon, and if his weapon is a fetich of some order or other, so is mine!" He pulled a queer object surreptitiously from his pocket and handed it across. "Pocket piece," he offered laconically. "Had the fool thing for years; just seemed to hang onto it, you know, but it's sure proved its usefulness."

McLaughlin studied it closely. A round, gold disk it was, embossed with a supine figure, over which, in an attitude of hostility, knelt a second figure. "And it is——"

Whiting grinned sheepishly. "A trophy of football days. Represents the boy's idea of my prowess on the gridiron; but now, under stress of circumstances, it has attained a higher responsibility and is the mu-zanyu's—white man's—all-powerful fetich. Through it comes the knowledge that the Goddess of Fire shall lead us, a few at a time perhaps, into a land more wonderful than any dream, wherein the wild beast and man live peaceably together, and at the end of a certain time, which is still more wonderful, man will be given a mysterious power by which he will be able to conquer perhaps even the Goddess herself. And though partly indistinct it further hints of a coming power great enough to conquer—— Oh, anything!"

"You told those natives that?" McLaughlin's face was a study, his tone incredulous.

"Yes; and, what's more, she's to make us a formal call; likely to-day. You know she will, Mack. I'll bet she's wild with curiosity right now."

"Of course, Dunk, you meant all right, but you understand an overdose of imagination is a bad thing sometimes. The situation is far too grave to be mastered by a trifling bit of untruthful strategy, and if she does come back—as I'm positive she will sooner or later—it will not be to lead us gently into the inner circle of her domestic shrine, and those natives will soon find it out. No; I'm afraid it'll make things worse."

But Whiting was obdurate. "It will at least give us a chance to get our bearings," he argued, "and perhaps by that time—who knows?—I may have another inspiration. Anyway," he supplemented, "don't haggle at the quality of the straw you're offered in a pinch."

McLaughlin handed back the "fetich," and threw up his hands. "You're too convincing, Dunk. It's up to you when the time comes. You'd have made an "a No. 1" lawyer, but you've yet to explain the lady of yesterday, however. To me she still heads the list if our porters all are stolen or desert, and somehow I can't seem to make anything else matter—greatly."

Whiting rose and stretched himself, and from the movement he unconsciously cast care behind him. He also yawned prodigiously, as if very much pleased with himself and the world. "Give me time there, boy; don't push on the reins. I believe the quinine has at last held sacred rites over the one last fever germ, and I'm feelin' fine. If the old gentleman with the elasticity of countenance sees fit to furnish us a visit from that most gracious personage, his daughter, methinks I'll be in trim to receive her. At any rate, I'll further perpetrate that trimness by a morning's inventory of the lady's Tree-limb Avenue of last night."

McLaughlin smiled, and refused the invitation to accompany him. He wished to think, to discuss with himself, as he often did, the vagaries of life, and besides he felt quite positive there would be no telltale marks of the woman on the surface of the tree limbs.

He settled himself in the shade of a tree near the spring, and gave himself up to thought. He could hear the irrepressible Dunk calling back and forth to the porters, most of whom tagged at his heels, since he now held the power that was to afford them everlasting protection, and he wondered what the outcome would be when it was discovered that their confidence had been so ill-treated.

The voices grew distant. They were evidently making an extensive investigation, but the morning in itself mothered the idea. It was an unusual morning for this altitude in the tropics. The fog had disappeared, and the sun was bright against the wonderful blue of the sky, while little tufts of breezes threw down delicious odors from the lap of the forest and then scurried past themselves, as if inviting notice to their great achievements.

He found it hard to think anything but well of the world on such a morning as this, and yet he knew even now forces which he could not comprehend were at work in some mysterious manner that was not well, else where were his ten missing porters? And when not a half dozen yards away, across the gurgling mouth of the little spring, he saw what he felt positive was the answer to his question.

Painters have painted, poets have sung, and sculptors have carved in stone the real and the ideal beauties of nature for all time, but it yet remains for genius to recognize the repulsive as a thing that calls to his art in tones impressive enough to warrant a reproduction. And to McLaughlin, taking in every detail of the unreal object before him, there came the wonder as to why this should be. The thing was surely impressive enough.

Against the spring-willow green of a clump of underbrush it stood forth as vivid as a splendidly cut cameo, revealing every line, every detail with a clearness one might experience if looking through a powerful magnifying glass. He knew it for a human being —a woman, in fact—but in all his months of experiencing the most abject and degraded specimens of mankind, nothing in his memory could lay claim to such as this.

The body was almost devoid of covering, and the skin seemed gathered over the bones of what was an enormous framework in wrinkled folds and pleats —the effect apparently of age and exposure—while interspersing and partially covering these folds and pleats, on the upper portion of the body, was what had once been elaborate and profuse tattooing. Around the neck hung string after string of barbarous ornaments—a conglomeration of customs copied from a dozen tribes—while from a peculiarly wrought cincture—belt—around the waist suspended a meager apron of a skin that was unknown to the white man. Overtopping this, and above the wrinkled face, was a headdress incongruous and impossible, through which were scattered disks of beaten gold. Below this headdress the eyes burned out with an intensity wholly foreign to the average native, and spoke plainly of incidents beyond the usual channel of even the hazardous life of the tropic dweller.

Even as his eyes registered all this and his brain took note of it, the old woman salaamed profoundly and spoke in the tongue of the Dahomey-ite: "Is it that you are the White Moon god, who comes to conquer and perhaps kill?"

Her tone was low, but the ring of passionate sarcasm accompanying the words disputed the profundity of the courtesy, and a half snarl lent a hideous aspect to the lip-ringed mouth drawn taut across the yellow teeth.

McLaughlin had no thought of fear; instead he felt an invigorating thrill sweep over him.

The old woman took a step nearer. "Iluko, Goddess of Fire, then—— It is that you bring a message to her?" The words were more assertive than questioning.

"Perhaps," parried McLaughlin, looking her straight in the eyes. "Would it be possible now—er —perhaps Iluko will care to talk with me herself?"

For answer the woman parted the bushes and turned with a curt look of command to him. "Come, follow Alabie," was all she said.

McLaughlin obeyed.

TO BE CONTINUED.

Soldiers' and Sailors' Personal Relief Section

Conducted by a former officer of the Adjutant General's Department, U. S. Army

WE wish to announce that, due to the fact that so many soldiers and sailors are being discharged rapidly and are thus facing problems which prove difficult to handle, we are establishing this Section not only because we wish this magazine to be more than a publication containing the best fiction, but we want to help the man who has given up his all for the country.

We have secured the services of a former officer in the Adjutant General's Department of the U. S. Army. He has been in the service for two years, having handled personally all matters relating to War Risk Insurance, Allowances, Allotments, Military Law, Correspondence, and everything which relates to the problem of the man in uniform. He wishes to make this Section not only a valuable thing for the discharged man, but he would like to have those who still remain in the service use it as a convenient means to settle the various questions in their minds. For example: If a man has made an allotment, and his family did not receive their money, the former officer who conducts this Section will be glad to look into the case, and do what he can to clear it up. In the service he handled many thousands of such cases with success. Also the soldier or sailor frequently wonders why he doesn't get promoted or transferred or some other important detail of his life perplexes him which a helping hand might make much easier. We invite you to write whenever you desire to this Section, no matter whether you subscribe to the magazine or not. There will be no charge for the services rendered, and no limit to the number of times which we will be ready to do what we can for you.

The discharged man faces a great many more problems than his brother in service. Not only is it necessary for him to secure a position, but his mind must accustom itself to new conditions. The Government and many private agencies have established employment bureaus. It is not primarily the policy of this Section to take up the matter of employment. However, we will be glad to advise a man as to what he is best suited for if he writes us giving a complete description of his former occupations, and what he did in the army. The purpose of this Section is rather to help the discharged man put himself *mentally* upon his feet. This can be accomplished in many ways. The best way to our mind is to get down to brass tacks. In other words, a man returns to his home, and finds that conditions are materially changed. Old friends have gone away or died, sisters have married, brothers have taken up work in other places, and the sweetheart may have found another chap in the meanwhile—all making a kind of muddle which is confusing and disheartening to the chap who comes home. This is so largely a true condition of America at this time that such a section as this is not only a benefit but an absolute necessity. We want you to write to us confidentially, laying your entire problem before us and giving us an opportunity to see what we can do for you.

The directions to secure the services of this Section are very brief. Write plainly, not necessarily on the typewriter, and inclose a self-addressed and stamped envelope for reply. We will do the rest. There is no problem that we will ignore. If it is your problem, that is enough for us. As copy for the magazine must be sent to the composing room far in advance of the date of publication, the first questions sent in by persons reading this announcement cannot be printed in this department for four or five issues. So mail your problem right away, stating whether you wish it to be regarded confidentially or not. If it is not marked confidential, we will consider it as a general proposition and endeavor to give it space in this Section, so that we may help others. If it is confidential we will write to you directly, and see that your problem does not reach any one but yourself. Don't stand on ceremony. As we say in the Army, come across. If you have a good thing, use it. This is a practical working proposition—something organized and planned for a direct reason. We want to help the soldier and sailor in every way that we can. We have heard so much about the various endeavors to assist him in securing employment that we thought that a Section devoted to his personal or mental problems might be of tremendous assistance in an hour of need. If you have got something on your "chest," get it off. Sit right down this minute and write to us, and tell us your whole story.

"Around the World"

Finds Four Human Skeletons in Cave.

The finding of four perfectly preserved skeletons, some Mexican coins of ancient date, two flint and steel rifles, pieces of broken pottery of Indian make, a tomahawk, and some stone arrowheads in a cave among the cliffs of the Devil's River, thirty miles from Menard, Texas, probably solves the mystery of the disappearance of several pioneers of the West during the early sixties.

Old-timers declare that from their fathers they learned that more than a dozen venturesome spirits who decided to explore the regions lying in the wilds of the Devil's River country in those days were never seen after they left the outskirts of the little village.

At that time it was believed they perished in some dismal swamp, on some desert, or were devoured by wild beasts. It is now believed they were captured by roving bands of Indians, taken to the cave, robbed and tortured to death or left to starve by their captors.

The cave is located in an isolated and barren rock formation high above the river. It was discovered by John H. Hall, who was hunting deer in the neighborhood and was forced to take refuge among the rocks during a terrific storm.

Hall at that time explored only a small section of the vast expanse which lay beyond the mouth where he was sheltered from the elements. He discovered one of the skeletons, however, and brought the news back to Menard. Later in the week a party of several citizens, headed by the sheriff, went to the cave and made a partial exploration of it, discovering the remaining skeletons, guns, et cetera.

One of the skeletons was found some fifty feet from the entrance of the cave. This was in the hallway leading to a main room. In the large room was found three skeletons. They lay but a few feet apart, which caused the explorers to believe the persons were tied to the jagged rocks and left to die, the skeletons falling forward when the material, used in binding the men, decayed.

A round hole in the skull of the skeleton found in the hallway led to the belief that this man was murdered by the Indians and dragged into the cave.

That the rifles were the property of the men dying in the cave is accepted as a matter of fact. They had lain so long on the floor that when they were touched the wooden parts crumbled. Bits of earthenware made the party making the discovery believe Indians once used the cave as their dwelling.

The Mexican coins bore the date of the sixties, and Mexican money in this section then was more plentiful than that of the United States. The presence of a tomahawk indicates that the cave was used by Indians long before Mexico was a republic.

Old settlers say they were told by their parents of Indian raids and of the bad feeling between pioneers and marauding redskin bands.

The sheriff believes the skeletons are those of bandits who were numerous in the West before the Civil War. He thinks these men were driven to the cave and besieged until they starved. Others believe the men were murdered by cattle thieves and their bodies placed in the cave.

Halted by Ghosts on Way to Work.

John Ingersoll, a coal miner who makes his home in Petersburg, Ind., is anxious to know whether ghosts are trailing him or whether he has been singled out for the pranks of a pair of human jokers who go to considerable trouble to carry out their grim designs. According to a story related by Ingersoll he met with a most startling and uncommon experience at four o'clock on a recent morning while on his way to the Blackburn mines, located three miles north of Petersburg.

Ingersoll always walks to the mine and follows the railroad track. His duties necessitate his being at the mine at an early hour. On the morning in question, he was about one mile from the city, when two tall ghostly figures, both in white and with white, ghastly faces, waved their long arms at him, as if commanding him to halt. He did halt, not knowing what else to do, as he never had had any experience in combating ghosts.

The two white figures advanced to the middle of the roalroad tracks, approaching him noiselessly and, forming an arch by joining their hands, one of the figures motioned to him with its head, as much as to say, "Pass through."

It was still quite dark, and as Ingersoll passed through the arch and turned about he was amazed, he says, to see the eyes in both ghastly faces suddenly illuminated by a bright yellow light that resembled flaming fire. He then took to his heels, but turned several times to see if he was being followed. He was not, but the two specters, each time he looked back, pointed at him with long fingers and arms, as if marking him for some impending disaster.

Ingersoll related his strange story to several of the coal miners, and suggested that it might be a joke, perpetrated by two fellows clad in sheets and with electric flash lights concealed beneath their covering. The other miners, he says, were not inclined to laugh over the affair. The majority of them were inclined to be superstitious, one of them remarking: "I've been a miner over twenty years, and have seen strange things happen, and worse things follow. What you saw was a vision, I should say, a warning of danger and possible death, and take it from me ye had better watch out."

No practical jokers having come to light to twit Ingersoll of his timidity, the puzzled miner says he will take his companion's advice and be prepared for what may come. Ingersoll is not a drinking man and generally spends his time at home when not working in the mine.

Fishermen Sail Six Hours Through Hot Sea.

That a large area of the sea lying north of the South American coast and southeast of the West Indies is now a seething mass of boiling water from which clouds of vapor rise and which hinder navigation, and the temperature of which is hot enough to cook eggs and spoil cargoes of fish, is the remarkable story brought to Freeport, Texas, by Captain Isaac Gorman of the fishing smack *Isabel*.

Captain Gorman declares that he sailed for six hours through the boiling seas, and that during that time his cargo of several thousand pounds of fish spoiled and had to be dumped overboard. He also says sailors on the *Isabel* cooked eggs in the sea as his vessel passed through the boiling waters, and that life on the ship became almost unbearable because of the extreme heat and the nauseating stench which filled the air.

"We struck the boiling waters when some six hundred miles from our port," said Captain Gorman. "We had captured a large amount of fish, and since our ice was limited were making all speed for home. Early one morning I noticed clouds of vapor rising straight ahead. The heat became more apparent. We thought the vapor was but a fog which we frequently find in that part of the sea—and sailed into it.

"As we struck the area overhung by vapor we learned our mistake. Instead of being an ordinary fog and an ordinary sea, we found we were sailing through boiling water. Thinking that a small area had become affected by volcanic action we steered ahead and continued to so steer, believing every moment that we were about to clear the seething seas, until we covered almost one hundred miles.

"During our passage through this boiling area the entire cargo of the *Isabel* was ruined. The waters so heated the sides and bottom of the vessel that the fish rotted and the stench added to the odor from the sea made many of the sailors sick. We were compelled to dump the cargo overboard and return home empty.

"During our run through these boiling waters—about six hours—several of the men on board dipped small sacks of eggs into the sea. These were cooked in short time. Sailors drew water up in buckets and found it to be heated to a high degree."

Captain Gorman declares he has sailed the gulf for thirty years and never saw anything like the discovery he has just made, nor experienced anything like what he has just gone through.

He says this particular section of the gulf is thoroughly charted, but is little used. In fact, it was the first time he ever crossed it, because it is known to be a part of the gulf where seaweeds and other matter sometimes gather to such extent that navigation is hampered. He would not have made the trip across this section but for the fact that he was compelled to rush home to save his cargo and it furnished a shorter route.

Captain Gorman does not believe the boiling waters have been there forever. He thinks this heated area is due to volcanoes or some natural phenomena. But he says that if it is found that the seas there have been boiling hot for a number of years, the mystery of the origin of tropical hurricanes is solved.

As for Captain Gorman, further investigations of the startling discovery will not be pushed. He says that he would not cross that area of the gulf again for any money, nor will he sail the *Isabel* anywhere near it. If he did, he would go alone, for the sailors on his boat say they have had enough of that part of the sea to last them for eternity.

One of the sailors, Peter Schmidt by name, more superstitious than others, declares he prayed the whole time they were crossing the boiling area. He is firmly convinced that this part of the gulf, this strange area of boiling water where stifling vapors fill the air and nothing of animal life exists, is nothing more or less than hell itself. Schmidt declares he plainly saw imps of hell floating in the vapors, and that they were grasping, stabbing, and clutching at the men on the vessel. Other members of the crew do not share Schmidt's opinion, though they declare the water is hot enough to accommodate the purposes of Satan.

Grave Pilferers Caught.

The Paris newspaper public dearly loves a crime tinged by the morbid and the horrible. A series of burglaries committed in the cemetery of Pere-Lachaise has provided columns of reading matter for some time past, particularly since the criminals have been identified as persons of a fairly high order of intelligence. One of them is a sculptor, another a painter, while a woman accomplice is a popular singer in the cabarets of Belleville. Between them they have violated seventy tombs since December 15, 1913, and have disposed of thousands of dollars' worth of rings taken from the bodies of the dead, and sacred images and vases removed from the vaults of well-known families.

The police, as well as the watchmen in Pere-Lachaise, knew that a daring band was operating almost every night in the cemetery. But they were unable to catch them red-handed. A huge police dog that was turned loose immediately after the closing of the gates rendered no assistance in tracking the mysterious intruders. One morning a priest entered the chapel of the cemetery to say a very early morning mass. He missed a massive silver vase, and noticed the poor box, broken and rifled, on the floor. The thieves had evidently just departed, for he found a rope still dangling from one of the windows opening toward the cemetery wall. A few nights later a man was seen scaling the wall at about the same spot, but he slipped away before the arrival of the police.

Taking the location of the point of entry as a clew, detectives made a careful search through the cafés of the Place Gambetta. Suspicion eventually fell upon Fournier, sculptor of funereal monuments and a man of marked ability, and Louis Geslin, a blacksmith who paints pictures and composes songs in his spare time. These two men were overheard talking in a bar about the location, in Pere-Lachaise, of certain well-known graves. They were shadowed, and it was learned that Fournier spent a good deal of his time in the cemetery. He told the attendants that he was studying the monuments for professional reasons. One day, however, he was observed to mark several graves by carelessly dropping cough lozenges on the headstones. The following morning two of the graves so marked had been violated.

The arrest of the suspects quickly followed. Geslin's mistress, Germaine Servert, was found wearing a silver cross that had been stolen from the mausoleum of the Hauboy family, and was also taken into custody. Still another male accomplice, a deserter from the military aviation service, has been run down; but these are believed to be only four of a gang of twelve or fourteen persons. The ringleader and brains of the bands is undoubtedly the marble worker, Camille Fournier. It was he who familiarized himself with every nook and corner of Pere-Lachaise and instructed his fellow ghouls how and when to break into a vault.

A search through the pawnshops and secondhand jewelry stores has brought many of the stolen objects to light. One dealer in antiquities has confessed that after buying a silver statuette of the Virgin from a stranger, he recognized it as being a relic from a tomb in Pere-Lachaise and threw it into the Seine to avoid detection. The thieves proved that they knew what they were about, for they took valuable objects only, and disposed of nearly all of them. It is now believed that the same gang was responsible for the revolting profanation of the grave of the actress, Mademoiselle Lantelme, in December, 1911, when a large haul of rings and other valuables was made.

Finds Queer Race in Malay.

The Malayan correspondent of a Rangoon newspaper has discovered the Panggang. This is not a variety of tea, a brand of rice, or the last word in firecrackers, as the reader could not be blamed for thinking. It is a race of human beings descended—who knows!—from one of the lost ten tribes of Israel, or the legendary nomads who emigrated from Central Asia before the era of Greek Civilization.

The Panggang have many eccentric customs. They wander through the dense jungles of the northern part of the Malay Peninsula, never stopping long enough in one place to need a police department or a board of aldermen. They sleep where night finds them, with the root of a tree as a pillow and a single huge palm leaf as a bed quilt. They neither fight nor steal, and have no use for money. If by chance they get hold of English or Siamese coins, they bury them in order that their spirits may have the wherewithal for trading after death.

Their vices are few. They do not chew gum, but are slaves to tobacco and salt; the last named takes the place of candy with this benighted race. They will remain for days without food, as long as they have a large supply of tobacco and salt. In the meat line, they will eat monkey, snake, elephant, or tiger, but are particularly partial to wild pig.

The Panggang marriage rites have been reduced to first principles. The prospective bride is given a start of one lap around a big ant hill, and the bridegroom does his best to catch her. He usually succeeds, but if he is absolutely hopeless as a sprinter and collapses before she does, the marriage is declared off amid the jeers of the spectators. These people do not appear to have any religion, but have a vague theory regarding the transmigration of souls. An exceptionally worthy Panggang is promoted after death to be a tiger.

But the Malay journalist touches high-water mark in his account of a mysterious female named Toh Medang, who is honored as a sort of queen and whose prime minister is a tame Wa-Wa which is a species of orang-utan. Toh Medang is reputed to be a great enchantress. She lives alone in a bamboo hut, shaded by the leaves of the sa red Ubang tree. Special food is brought to her every day by the oldest man or woman of the neighborhood, accompanied by the latest-born infant. The Panggangs believe that she could bring awful calamities upon them if they incurred her displeasure. With this reputation to live up to, she is careful never to leave her hut, but sends the tame Wa-Wa to funerals as her proxy.

Mathematical Cop.

If the Paris gendarme, Costy, were a member of the police force in the United States, he would be known as the "Rapid Calculator," or possibly as the "Mathematical Cop." For Costy, thirty-six years old and a guardian of the peace for eleven years to the complete satisfaction of his superior officers, is endowed with an extraordinary genius for figures. The daily routine has prevented him from exploring the mysteries of the higher mathematics, but he has developed an extraordinary ability to tell, the moment he hears a phrase uttered, exactly how many letters the various words contain. Lately this has become an obsession with him.

When one speaks to Costy his first idea is not to understand what has been said, but to count. Words no longer have meanings for him; they are merely conglomerations of letters. He counts in spite of himself, and is beginning to be seriously worried lest his fatal gift should render him useless as a servant of the public.

"The Paris policemen are fine fellows," said an American to him the other day.

"Thirty-one," murmured Costy in reply. He simply could not help it, for he had perceived in an instant that thirty-one letters had gone to make up the phrase.

It is reported that he heard two workmen quarreling in the street.

"Bandit!" roared one.

"Madman!" shrieked the other, shaking a horny fist.

Costy hurried up to arbitrate. "It is six of one and half a dozen of the other," he announced as he separated the noisy fellows and sent them on their way. The crowd cheered this decision, but they did not realize the full extent of Costy's sagacity. If they had thought for a moment they would have realized that the opprobrious terms, "Bandit" and "Madman" each contain six letters.

This otherwise normal policeman can no longer read the newspaper with any satisfaction. He counts the letters in the headlines instead of informing himself as to the most recent events in Mexico. He cannot even take ordinary human pleasure in a letter from his best girl. Numbers prevent him from eating, from sleeping in peace. He is so worried over his present state of mind that he has asked his chief to submit his case to competent scientists.

Says Earth is on Wane.

According to Monsieur Veronnet of the Astronomical Society of France, we are standing to-day at the exact middle, and therefore at the highest point, of the curve representing terrestrial existence. He figures that the earth is two million years old. Consequently it has two million more years to live. Up to the present moment, it has been growing, evolving; hereafter, it will decline. By slow degrees animal and plant life will disappear. The ocean will evaporate, and the globe will be reduced to the condition of a vast burned-out ember whirling through space.

Cold will be the agency to bring about this depressing result. This is by no means a new theory, but Monsieur Veronnet has worked it out on a mathematical basis and the Astronomical Society is inclined to take him seriously. He believes that the sun has begun to contract. In two million years' time it will not be throwing off enough heat to support life on this planet. The energy in a ray of sunlight will be only one-tenth what it is at present. The temperature will never go above freezing point and the earth will eventually become frozen to the core. This universal death will probably be preceded among human beings by a return to barbarism.

The same fate has already overtaken Mars and all the planets farther removed from the sun than we are. Speculations about the character and appearance of the Martians are therefore idle. There are no Martians, though Venus, being still in the tropical belt, may be peopled by living beings. The scientist does not state how long it will be before Venus, too, is frozen out, but with the earth's two million years' lease of life to go upon, it ought to be a simple problem for any schoolboy.

Find Hieroglyphic Slab in Coal Mine.

William Posey and Ed Sturgeon, two coal miners who work in the Atlas coal mines just north of Petersburg, Ind., made a valuable discovery that is of considerable interest to hieroglyphic students throughout the country.

The boys were working a rift of coal when one noticed a peculiar piece of coal that resembled a slab of wood. They carefully picked it out and found it to contain many hieroglyphic figures, drawn in straight lines.

In the same mine miners have found petrified fish, forest leaves, and ocean shells. The recent find was made at a depth of one hundred and twelve feet beneath the surface of the earth, eighty feet of which was solid sandstone and rock.

Says Masked "Chicken" "Copped" His Jewelry.

When is a chicken not a chicken? When she takes off her mask.

That, at least, is the way Louis Biess has it doped out, following an experience which resulted in his asking the police to locate "May," aged forty-eight, weight one hundred and ninety pounds, five feet five inches in height, and with white hair.

May, he says, has his purse, containing two hundred and twenty-five dollars' worth of jewelry, thirty-five dollars in cash, and a check for one hundred dollars.

Biess lunched in a restaurant at Colma. As he was about to leave a friendly waiter stepped up and whispered:

"That chicken out there in the flu mask is waiting for a street car. I think she'd go with you in your automobile if you are going to San Francisco."

"Some eyes!" murmured Biess. "I'll ask her."

"Sure," was the masked beauty's response to his invitation, and a moment later they were speeding for the city.

As they neared their destination a vagrant wind blew off the "chicken's" low-worn hat and disarranged her mask.

Biess was polite, but he didn't waste time in long-drawn-out farewells.

Later he discovered his purse was missing.

"All is not gold that glitters behind a flu mask," said Biess in reporting the theft. "And a flu mask may cover a multitude of sins. Now if that mask ordinance had only been called off yesterday instead of to-day—but what's the use?"

Sues Barber Who Put Lather in His Mouth.

Aleck Koonrad, of Flanders, N. Y., entered the Palace Tonsorial Parlor, seated himself in a chair, and announced that he wanted a shave. Barber Whaley had his customer nearly lathered when Koonrad coughed, opened his mouth, and gasped. Whaley stuck the brush, which was covered with lather, into Koonrad's wide-open mouth. Koonrad jumped from the chair and claimed Whaley did it to be mean. The barber denied the accusation.

Koonrad later went to the barber shop and demanded one hundred dollars from Whaley as a settlement for damages. Whaley refused to pay.

Now Koonrad has commenced a court action. In his complaint he alleges that the lather made him sick to his stomach, that he had a violent headache, and could not eat for two days.

In his answer Whaley states that he had the brush on Koonrad's upper lip, and that when he coughed the brush slipped into Koonrad's mouth; that it was not his fault, and had Koonrad not gasped it would not have happened.

The case will be tried before Judge Black and a jury next week.

Needle in Man's Body Fifty Years.

J. S. Allgood, a prominent farmer of Yazoo County, Miss., reports a unique experience.

For some time Mr. Allgood, who is in his fifty-second year, has been complaining of his back hurting him. He would suddenly feel stinging pains in that part of his body, and was at a loss to account for such visitations, as otherwise he was in good health.

A short time ago, while out inspecting his fine drove of registered Duroc hogs, he suddenly felt a sharp pain in the lower section of his back bone. On reaching around to rub the ailing spot his hand came in contact with the sharp point of what proved to be a needle sticking out of his flesh. He seized hold of the needle's point and pulled it out.

Upon comparing it with other needles in his home, it was found to be of an old-fashioned pattern like those that he remembered were used in the South following the Civil War. This leads him to believe that the needle must have entered his body when he was an infant, and remained there over fifty years.

Mr. Allgood explains that he was born and raised in Georgia, and while he had heard of certain Georgia people feeding their small children clay and small bits of flint rock, he declares he never heard of any Georgians feeding their babies steel needles.

www.ingramcontent.com/pod-product-compliance
Lightning Source LLC
Chambersburg PA
CBHW081148170626
46809CB00010B/3145